PURITY OF BLOOD

ARTURO PÉREZ-REVERTE is the internationally bestselling author of *The Queen of the South* and *Captain Alatriste*. He lives near Madrid, Spain.

PURITY
OF BLOOD

Arturo Pérez-Reverte

TRANSLATED FROM THE SPANISH BY
Margaret Sayers Peden

A PLUME BOOK

PLUME
Published by Penguin Group
Penguin Group (USA) Inc., 375 Hudson Street, New York, New York 10014, U.S.A.
Penguin Group (Canada), 90 Eglinton Avenue East, Suite 700, Toronto, Ontario, Canada
M4P 2Y3 (a division of Pearson Penguin Canada Inc.)
Penguin Books Ltd., 80 Strand, London WC2R 0RL, England
Penguin Ireland, 25 St. Stephen's Green, Dublin 2, Ireland (a division of Penguin Books Ltd.)
Penguin Group (Australia), 250 Camberwell Road, Camberwell, Victoria 3124, Australia
(a division of Pearson Australia Group Pty. Ltd.)
Penguin Books India Pvt. Ltd., 11 Community Centre, Panchsheel Park, New Delhi –
110 017, India
Penguin Books (NZ), cnr Airborne and Rosedale Roads, Albany, Auckland 1310,
New Zealand (a division of Pearson New Zealand Ltd.)
Penguin Books (South Africa) (Pty.) Ltd., 24 Sturdee Avenue, Rosebank, Johannesburg 2196,
South Africa

Penguin Books Ltd., Registered Offices: 80 Strand, London WC2R 0RL, England

Published by Plume, a member of Penguin Group (USA) Inc. Previously published in a
Putnam edition.

First Plume Printing, December 2006
10 9 8 7 6 5 4 3 2 1

Copyright © Arturo Pérez-Reverte, 1997
English translation copyright © Margaret Sayers Peden, 2006
All rights reserved

 REGISTERED TRADEMARK—MARCA REGISTRADA

The Library of Congress has catalogued the Putnam edition as follows:

Pérez-Reverte, Arturo.
[Limpieza de sangre. English]
    Purity of blood / Arturo Pérez-Reverte ;
    translated from the Spanish by Margaret Sayers Peden.
        p.   cm.
    ISBN 0-399-15320-9 (hc.)
    ISBN 0-452-28798-7 (pbk.)
    I. Peden, Margaret Sayers.   II. Title.
    PQ6666.E765L5613   2006   2005050984
    863'.64—dc22

Printed in the United States of America
Original hardcover design by Marysarah Quinn

For Carlota,

for whom there is no choice

but to fight . . .

Glory and honor blazoned on the quarters
of the escutcheon, hidalgos, poets, priests,
fabulous Americas, ladies-in-waiting,

galleys that apprehend the infidel,
gibbets by the roadside, adventures,
and swords flashing on every corner.

TOMÁS BORRÁS,
Castilla

PURITY OF BLOOD

I. SEÑOR QUEVEDO'S
DIFFICULT MOMENT

That day there were bullfights in the Plaza Mayor, but constable Martín Saldaña's festive fire had been doused. A woman had been found in a sedan chair in front of the church of San Ginés, strangled. In her hand was a pouch containing fifty *escudos* and a handwritten, unsigned note bearing the words, *For masses for your soul.*

A pious old woman on her way to early church had found the body. She advised the sacristan, and he had informed the parish priest who, after a hurried absolution, *sub conditione,* made a report to the authorities. By the time the chief constable showed up to make his token appearance in the small plaza of San Ginés, local residents and curious bystanders were milling around the sedan chair. The chair and its contents had become the object of a local pilgrimage, and a number of Saldaña's catchpoles were needed to hold back the crowd while the judge and the scribe drew up their documents and Martín Saldaña made his cursory examination of the corpse.

The chief constable set about his task in the most leisurely fashion, as if he had time to burn. Perhaps it was because of his history as a former soldier—he had served in Flanders before his wife (at least it was said it had been she) obtained his present position for him. In any case, Madrid's chief constable went about his duties at a pace that a certain satiric poet—the gifted-in-wealth-as-well-as-talent Ruiz de Villaseca—had described in a poisonous *décima* as *paso de buey*, an ox's pace. It was a clear allusion to the lethargy with which the chief constable picked up his staff of office, or attempted to parry the staffs his wife welcomed.

In any case, if it is true that Martín Saldaña was slow in certain things, he was definitely not so when it came to drawing his sword, or dagger, or poniard, or the well-oiled pistols he was wont to wear in his waistband—all of which clanged like sounds issuing from a smithy. On the night of the third day after the aforementioned *décima* had circulated among the gossipers gathered at the *mentidero* of San Felipe, the most popular of Madrid's rumor mills, this same now-not-so-gifted Villaseca had been found at the very door to this house with three sword-tailored buttonholes in his body. He was now extremely well qualified—

whether from Purgatory, Hell, or wherever—to confirm exactly how swiftly the constable could move.

The fact is that from the calm and collected inspection the head constable made of the cadaver, almost nothing was learned. The dead woman was mature, nearer fifty than forty, dressed in a voluminous black gown and a head-dress that lent her the look of a duenna, or a lady's companion. Her purse held a rosary, along with a key and a crumpled religious card depicting the Virgin of Atocha. Around the victim's neck was a gold chain bearing a medallion of Saint Águeda. Her own features suggested that in her younger days she had been well favored. There were no signs of violence other than the silk cord still cutting into her neck, and her mouth, frozen in the rictus of death. From her color, and the rigor, the constable concluded that she had been strangled the preceding night, in that same sedan chair, before being carried to church.

The detail of the pouch with money for masses for her soul indicated a twisted sense of humor—or, conversely, great Christian charity. After all, in the dark, violent, and contradictory Spain of our Catholic King Philip IV, in which dissolute wastrels and rough-living braggarts howled for confession at the top of their lungs after being shot or run through by a sword, it was not unusual to encounter a pious swordsman.

· · ·

Martín Saldaña told us about the event late that afternoon.
Or, to be more precise, told Captain Alatriste. We met him
at the Guadalajara gate, returning among the crowd from
the Plaza Mayor after he had completed his inquiries regarding the murdered woman. Her body had been laid out
in Santa Cruz in one of the coffins for hanged prisoners,
in hopes that someone might identify her. The constable
merely mentioned the murder in passing, more interested
in the performance of the afternoon's bulls; at that time in
Madrid, street crimes were common, but afternoons of
bulls and *cañas* were growing scarce.

Cañas, a kind of tourney on horseback between teams
of fine gentlemen, in which our lord and king himself
sometimes participated, had become very mannered—a
contest between pretty-boys and fops, tending more toward
flourishing and flirting and ladies than toward cracking
heads, as God would have it. They were not in any way
what they had been in days of the wars between the
Moors and the Christians, or even in the lifetime of our
young monarch's grandfather, the great Philip II. As for
the bulls, they were still, in that first third of the century,
a passion of the Spanish people. Of the more than seventy
thousand residents of Madrid, two thirds flocked to the
Plaza Mayor every time the bulls challenged the courage

and skill of the caballeros who confronted them. Because in those days, hidalgos, grandees of Spain, even men of royal blood, had no hesitation about riding out into the plaza on their finest steeds to bury the dagger-point of their *rejón*, the long wooden lance, in the withers of a fine Jarama bull. Or one of them might just as readily dismount and bring the bull down with his sword, amid the applause of the crowd that gathered either beneath the arches of the plaza—in the case of the common folk—or on balconies rented for as much as twenty-five or fifty *escudos* by courtiers and papal and foreign ambassadors.

These events were then celebrated in ballads and poems—either elegant, or comic and grotesque—events that Madrid's cleverest minds quickly seized upon to sharpen their wit. Such as the time a bull chased a constable, and the public took the side of the bull—officers of the law did not then, as they do not today, enjoy great popular favor; and:

The bull had good reason that day
to pursue the object of mirth,
for of the four horns in the fray
only two had been there at birth.

On one occasion the Admiral of Castile, while fighting, on horseback, an unusually large bull, accidentally wounded the Conde de Cabra instead of the beast. That was cause for the following famous lines—turning on the pun of the name Cabra, which means "goat"—to race through the most busily buzzing *mentideros* of Madrid.

A thousand and more have won fame,
but only the Admiral, abra-cadabra,
is the first, with his trusty lance,
to turn a bull into a Cabra.

It is understandable, then, returning to that Sunday of the murdered woman, that Martín Saldaña would bring Diego Alatriste up-to-date on what had kept him away from the afternoon's sport. The captain, in turn, recounted the details of the bullfights, which Their Majesties, the king and queen, had witnessed from the balcony of the Casa de la Panadería—and the captain and I standing among the ordinary public, eating piñon nuts and lupin seeds in the shade of the Pañeros arch.

There had been four bulls, all fiery; and both the Conde de Puñoenrostro and the Conde de Guadalmedina had been outstanding in placing their *rejones*. A Jarama bull had killed the latter count's horse, and he, very brave, very much the cavalier, had jumped to the ground, slashed the animal's tendons, and dispatched it with two good thrusts of his sword. That feat had earned a fluttering of ladies' fans, the approval of the king, and a smile from the queen—who, as word later had it, scarcely had taken her eyes off him, for Guadalmedina was a fine figure of a man.

The final bull added a last colorful note when it attacked the royal guard. As you may know, Your Mercies, three units of guardsmen—Spanish, German, and one of harquebusiers—always stood in formation below the royal box, lined up shoulder to shoulder and with halberds at the ready. They were forbidden to break rank, even should a bull charge them with all the animus of a Turk. That afternoon the snorting animal had made straight for the guards, bothered not a whit by the halberds, and had taken with him on a tour of the ring, impaled upon a wicked horn, one of the large blond Germans. The hapless guard found himself being separated from his innards amidst a chorus of *Himmel*s and *Mein Gott*s. Sacraments were administered there in the plaza.

"He was slipping around on his own guts, like that lieutenant in Ostend," Diego Alatriste concluded. "You remember him? The one in our fifth assault on the del Caballo redoubt . . . Ortiz was his name. Or Ruiz. Something like that."

Martín Saldaña nodded, stroking his graying beard, which he wore partly to hide the scar he had received twenty years before, around the third or fourth year of the century, during that same attack on the walls of Ostend.

They had poured out of the trenches at the break of dawn—Saldaña, Alatriste, and five hundred other men, among them my father, Lope Balboa. They'd swarmed the terreplein, with Captain Tomás de la Cuesta in the lead, followed closely by that lieutenant Ortiz, or Ruiz—oh, what the devil was he called?—carrying the flag bearing the cross of Saint Andrew.

Before climbing over the parapet, they had taken the first line of the Dutchmen's trenches with nothing but small arms, under constant enemy fire from above. They had spent half an hour in hand-to-hand fighting as musket fire whizzed around them. That was where Martín Saldaña had received the slash across his face and Diego Alatriste the one above his left eyebrow. Lieutenant Ortiz-Ruiz was hit by a musket ball fired at point-blank range, blowing away half his belly. His intestines spilled out and dragged on the ground and he struggled to hold them in with both hands as he ran to escape the battle. He did not have the chance, because almost immediately he was killed by a shot to the head.

Finally, Captain de la Cuesta, himself as bloody as an Ecce Homo, had said, "Caballeros, we have done all we can; let any man who can save his hide." My father and another short, tough soldier from Aragon, one Sebastián Copons, had helped Saldaña and Diego Alatriste get back to the Spanish trenches, with every Dutchman in the world firing at them from the walls. As they ran, they cursed God and the Virgin, or commended themselves to them, which in such cases was one and the same thing. And still someone had the time and fortitude to pick up poor Ortiz-Ruiz's banner rather than leave it on the bulwarks of the heretics, along with his corpse and those of two hundred comrades who were not going on into Ostend, or back to the trenches—or anywhere at all.

"Ortiz, I think it was," Saldaña concluded finally.

They had, a good year later, avenged the lieutenant and the two hundred other men, as well as those who left their hides in earlier, or later, assaults upon the Dutch del Caballo redoubt. Finally, after the eighth or ninth attempt, Saldaña, Alatriste, Copons, my father, and the other veterans of the Tercio Viejo de Cartagena, succeeded in battling their way inside the walls on the strength of nothing but bollocks. The Dutch began shouting *Srinden, srinden,* which I think means "friends," or "comrades," and then something that sounded like *Veijiven ons over*: "We surrender." And that was when Captain de la Cuesta, who was deaf to any foreign tongue but who had a stupendous memory, said, "We do not understand your *srinden* or *veijiven*— or anything your whoring mothers taught you—but we will show no mercy, you hear that? Not one heretic left alive." And when Diego Alatriste and the others at last raised the shredded, battle-worn cross of Saint Andrew above the bulwarks—the very same one poor Ortiz had carried before departing this world tangled in his own guts—they were drenched in the Dutch blood dripping from the blades of their daggers and swords.

"Someone told me you are going back," Saldaña said, after he had brought us up-to-date.

"I may."

Although I was still dazzled by the bulls, my eyes were filled with the people pouring out of the plaza and along Calle Mayor: Fine ladies and gentlemen rapped out "Fetch my coach" and then climbed into their carriages and rode away, and caballeros on horseback, and elegant courtiers headed toward San Felipe or the flagstone courtyard of the palace. At the time, I listened very carefully to the chief constable's words. In that year of 1623, the second in the reign of our young King Philip, the war in Flanders had resumed, creating the need for more money, more *tercios*, and more men. General Ambrosio Spínola was recruiting soldiers throughout Europe, and hundreds of veterans were hurrying to enlist under their old flags. The Tercio de Cartagena, decimated at Julich at the time my father was killed, and totally annihilated a year later in Fleurus, was being re-formed. Soon it would be following the Camino Español, a familiar route to the Low Countries, to play a part in the siege of the stronghold of Breda—or

Bredá, as we called it then. Although the wound Diego Alatriste had received in Fleurus had not completely healed, I was aware that he had been in contact with old comrades, with the intent of returning to its ranks. In recent days, the captain had made his living as a sword for hire, and despite that—or precisely because of it—he had made some powerful enemies at court. It would not be a bad idea to put some distance between them and him for a time.

"It might be for the best." Saldaña looked at Alatriste meaningfully. "Madrid has become dangerous. Will you take the boy?"

We were walking among a crowd of people just passing the closed silver shops, heading in the direction of the Puerta del Sol. The captain looked at me quickly, and made an ambiguous gesture.

"He may be too young," he said.

Beneath the chief constable's thick mustache I could make out a smile. As I admired the butts of his gleaming pistols, the dagger, and the sword with the wide guard, all of which hung from the waist of his buffcoat—a padded defense against knifings received in the course of his duties—he had laid his broad, hard hand on my head. *That hand*, I thought, *might once have shaken my father's.*

"Not too young for some things, I believe." Saldaña's smile stretched wider, partly amused and partly devilish.

For he knew what I had done the night of the adventure of the two Englishmen. "And anyway, you were his age when you enlisted."

This was true. Nearly a long quarter of a century before, the second son of an old family, with no standing in the world, thirteen years old and barely in command of writing, the four skills of arithmetic, and a taste of Latin, Diego Alatriste had run away from both school and home. In those desperate straits he reached Madrid, and by lying about his age was able to enlist as a drummer boy in one of the *tercios* leaving for Flanders under the command of King Philip's heir, the infante Alberto.

"Those were different times," the captain protested.

He had stepped aside to allow two señoritas with the air of high-priced harlots to pass, escorted by their gallants. Saldaña, who seemed to know them, tipped his hat, not without obvious sarcasm, which triggered an irate look from one of the dandies. It was a look that vanished like magic when he saw all the iron the head constable was toting.

"You are right about that," said Saldaña provocatively. "Those were different times, and different men."

"And different kings."

The head constable, whose eyes were still on the women, turned to Alatriste with a slight start, and then shot a sideways glance at me.

"Come, Diego, do not say such things before the boy." He looked around, uneasy. "And do not compromise me, by Christ. Remember, I am the Law."

"I am not compromising you. I have never failed in my duty to my king, whoever he may be. But I have served three, and I tell you that there are kings, and there are kings."

Saldaña stroked his beard. "God help us."

"God or whoever your draw your comfort from."

The head constable gave me another uneasy glance before turning back to Alatriste. I observed that he had unconsciously rested one hand on the pommel of his sword.

"You wouldn't be looking for a quarrel, would you, Diego?" The constable, heavyset and strong but slightly shorter than the captain, stood a little straighter and stepped in front of Alatriste.

The captain did not answer. His gray-green eyes locked with Saldaña's, expressionless beneath the broad brim of his hat. The two men stared at each other, nose to nose, their old soldier's faces crisscrossed with fine wrinkles and scars. Some passersby stared at them with curiosity. In that turbulent, ruined, but still proud Spain—in truth, pride was all we had left in our pockets—no one took back a word lightly spoken, and even close friends were capable of knifing each other over an ill-timed comment or denial.

He spoke, he walked by, he looked,
rash, unguarded words resound,
once spoken, too late, in a trice
the meadow is a dueling ground.

Only three days before, right in the middle of Rúa Prado, the Marqués de Novoa's coachman had knifed his master six times because he had called him a lout, and fights over a "Move out of my way" were commonplace. So for an instant, I thought that the two of them might go at each other there in the street. But they did not. For if it is true that the constable was entirely capable—and he had proved it before—of putting a friend in prison, even blow off his head in the exercise of his authority, it is no less true that he had never raised the specter of the law against Diego Alatriste over personal differences. That twisted ethic was very typical of the era among belligerent men, and I myself, who lived in that world in my youth, as well as the rest of my life, can testify that in the most soulless scoundrels, rogues, soldiers, and hired swords, I had found more respect for certain codes and unwritten rules than in people of supposedly honorable condition. Martín Saldaña was such a man, and his quarrels and squabbles were settled with a sword, man to man, without hiding behind the authority of the king or any of his underlings.

But thanks to God, their exchange had been in quiet voices, without making a public stir or doing irreparable damage to the old, tough, and contentious friendship between the two veterans. At any rate, Calle Mayor after a *fiesta de toros,* with all Madrid packed into the streets, was no place for hot words, or steel, or anything else. So in the end, Saldaña let the air out of his lungs with a hoarse sigh. All of a sudden he seemed relaxed, and in his dark eyes, still directed at Captain Alatriste, I thought I glimpsed the spark of a smile.

"One day, Diego, you are going to end up murdered."

"Perhaps. If so, no one better to do it than you."

Now it was Alatriste who was smiling beneath his thick soldier's mustache. I saw Saldaña wag his head with comic distress.

"We would do well," he said, "to change the subject."

He had reached out with a quick, almost clumsy, gesture—at once rough and friendly—and jabbed the captain's shoulder.

"Come, then. Buy me a drink."

And that was that. A few steps farther on, we stopped at the Herradores tavern, which was filled, as always, with lackeys, squires, porters, and old women willing to be hired out as duennas, mothers, or aunts. A serving girl set two jugs of Valdemoro on the wine-stained table, which Alatriste and the head constable tossed down in a nonce, for their

verbal sparring had quickened their thirst. I, not yet fourteen, had to settle for a glass of water from the large jug,
since the captain never allowed me a taste of wine except
what we dipped our bread into at breakfast—there was
not always money for chocolate—or, when I was not well,
to restore my color. Although Caridad la Lebrijana, on the
sly, would sometimes give me slices of bread sprinkled
with wine and sugar, a treat to which I, a boy without
two coins to rub together to buy sweets, was greatly
addicted.

In regard to wine, the captain told me that I would
have plenty of time in my life to drink till I burst, if I
wished; that it was never too late for a man to do that,
adding that he had known too many good men who ended
up lost in the fumes of Bacchus's grapes.

He told me these things little by little, for as I've said,
Alatriste was a man of few words, and his silences often
said more than when he spoke aloud. The fact is that later,
when I, too, was a soldier—among many other things—
I sometimes did tip my jug too much. But I was always civil
when I was tippling, and in me it never became a vice—I
had others that were worse—but only an occasional stim-
ulus and diversion. And I believe that I owe my modera-
tion to Captain Alatriste, although he never preached that
homily by example. On the contrary, I well remember his
long, silent drinking bouts. Unlike other men, he did not

often have his wine in company, nor did his bottles make him jolly. His way of drinking was calm, deliberate, and melancholy. And when the wine began to take effect, he would close up like a clam and avoid his friends.

In truth, every time I remember him drunk, it was alone in our lodgings on Calle del Arcabuz, on the court-yard that opened to the back of the Tavern of the Turk. He would sit motionless before his glass, jug, or bottle, his eyes fixed on the wall where he hung his sword, dagger, and hat, as if contemplating images that only he and his obstinate silence could evoke. And by the way his mouth tightened beneath his veteran's mustache, I would take an oath that the images were not those a man contem-plates, or relives, gladly. If it is true that each of us car-ries his specters within him, those of Diego Alatriste y Tenorio were not servile or friendly or good company. But, as I heard him say once, shrugging his shoulders in the way that was so typical of him—half resignation and half indifference—an honorable man can choose the way and the place he dies, but no one can choose the things he remembers.

Activity at the *mentidero* of San Felipe was at its peak. The steps and terrace of the church facing Calle Mayor were an anthill: people chattering in groups, strolling around greeting acquaintances, elbowing their way to a place at the railing from which they could watch the coaches and crowds filling the street below in the stylized promenade they called the *rúa*. That was where Martín Saldaña bid us farewell. We were not, however, alone for long, for shortly thereafter we ran into El Tuerto Fadrique, the one-eyed apothecary at Puerta Cerrada, and Dómine Pérez; they, too had just come from the spectacle of the bulls, and were still praising them. In fact, it had been the *dómine* who had administered the sacraments to the German guard whose traveling papers had just been signed by the Jarama bull. The Jesuit was recounting all the details, telling how the queen, being young, and French, had turned pale and nearly swooned in the royal box, and how our lord and king had gallantly taken her hand to comfort her. However, instead of retiring, as many expected she would do, she had stayed on at the Casa de la Panadería. Her gesture was so appreciated by the public that when she and the king rose, signaling the end of the spectacle, they were favored with a warm ovation, to which Philip the Fourth, young and refined as he was, responded by doffing his hat.

I have already told Your Mercies, on a different occasion, that in the first third of the century, the people of Madrid, despite their natural fondness for mischief and malice, still harbored a certain naiveté in regard to such

royal gestures. It was an ingenuousness that time and disasters would replace with disillusion, rancor, and shame.
But at the time of this tale, our monarch was still a young
man, and Spain, although already corrupt, and with mortal ulcers eating her heart, maintained her appearance, all
her dazzle and politesse. We were still a force to be reck-
oned with, and would continue to be for some time, until
we bled the last soldier and the last *maravedí* dry. Holland
despised us; England feared us; the Turk was ever hover-
ing 'round; the France of Richelieu was gritting its teeth;
the Holy Father received our grave, black-clad ambassadors with caution; and all Europe trembled at the sight of
our *tercios*—still the best infantry in the world—as if the
rat-a-tat-tat of the drums came from the Devil's own drum-
sticks. And I, who lived through those years, and those that
came later, I swear to Your Mercies that in that century we
were still what no country had ever been before.

And when the sun that had shed its light on Tenoch-
titlán, Pavia, San Quintín, Lepanto, and Breda finally set,
the horizon glowed red with our blood—but also that of
our enemies. As it had that day in Rocroi when I left the
dagger Captain Alatriste had given me in the body of a
Frenchman. Your Mercies will agree that we Spanish should
have devoted all that effort and courage to building a decent nation, instead of squandering it on absurd wars, rogu-
ery, corruption, chimeras, and holy water. And that is very

true. But I am reporting how it was. And furthermore, not all peoples are equally rational in choosing their opportunities or their destinies, nor equally cynical in later justifying to History or to themselves what they have done. As for us, we were men of our century. We did not choose to be born and to live in that often miserable but sometimes magnificent Spain, it was our fate. But it was our Spain. And that is the unhappy *patria*—or whatever word they use nowadays—that like it or not I carry under my skin, in my weary eyes, and in my memory.

It is in that memory that I see, as if it were yesterday, don Francisco de Quevedo at the foot of the San Felipe steps. He was, as always, wearing strict black, except for the starched white collar and red cross of Santiago on the left side of his doublet. And although the afternoon was sunny, he had flung over his shoulders the long cape he wore to disguise his lameness, a dark cloak whose tail was lifted by the sheath of the sword upon which his hand rested so casually. He was talking with some acquaintances, hat in hand, when a lady's greyhound roaming nearby nosed close enough to brush his gloved right hand. The lady was standing by the footboard of her coach, conversing with two caballeros—and she was pretty. As the hound meandered by, don Francisco patted its head, at the same time sending a quick and courtly glance toward its mistress. The greyhound trotted back to her as if it were a messenger of the caress, and the lady rewarded the poet's tribute with a smile and a flutter of her fan, both received by don Francisco with a slight nod as he twisted his luxuriant mustache between thumb and forefinger.

Poet, swordsman, and highly celebrated wit at court, don Francisco was also a gallant man who enjoyed a reputation among the ladies. Stoic, lucid, caustic, courageous, elegant even with his limp, he was a man of goodwill despite his hot temper, generous with his friends and unyielding to his enemies. He could dispatch an adversary as easily with two quatrains as with a duel on de la Vega hill, enchant a lady with genteel courtesy and a sonnet, or surround himself with the philosophers, academicians, and learned men who treasured his entertaining witticisms and his company. The good don Miguel de Cervantes—the greatest genius of all time, no matter how those English heretics chirp on about their Shakespeare—had been seated at God's right hand seven years ago when he had put his foot in the stirrup and given up his soul to the one who gave it to him. But before he died, even Cervantes had called don Francisco an excellent poet and a compleat caballero in these famous verses:

The scourge of mindless poets, he will
at dagger point drive from Parnassus
all the evils we fear will o'ertake us.

That afternoon, Señor Quevedo was, as he was wont, passing time on the steps of San Felipe while *le tout* Madrid ambled along Calle Mayor after their afternoon of watching the bulls—an entertainment the poet did not greatly enjoy. When he saw Captain Alatriste, who was strolling with Dómine Pérez, El Tuerto Fadrique, and me, he politely excused himself to his companions. I had no inkling of how profoundly that chance meeting was going to affect us, putting all our lives in danger—particularly mine—nor how fate delights in sketching bizarre designs with men's fortunes. If, as don Francisco came toward us with his usual affable expression that afternoon, someone had told us that the mystery of the dead woman was going to involve us in some way, the smile with which Captain Alatriste greeted the poet would have frozen on his lips. But one never knows how the dice will fall, and they are always cast before anyone even notices.

"I have a favor to ask of you," said don Francisco.

Between Señor Quevedo and Captain Alatriste, those words were a pure formality. That was obvious in the look, almost a reproach, the captain gave Quevedo in response. We had taken our leave of the Jesuit and the apothecary, and were now in the Puerta del Sol, walking past the awnings of the stalls around the fountain at the Buen Suceso church. The idle liked to sit on its rim and listen to the water playing, or gaze toward the façade of the church and the royal hospital. The captain and his friend were walking ahead of me, side by side, and I remember how they blended into and then emerged from the crowd in the fading light of dusk, the poet in his usual dark clothing, with his cape folded over his arm, and by his side, the captain in a brown doublet, modest square collar, and nicely fitting hose, his sword and dagger, as always, at his waist.

"I am greatly obliged, don Francisco, that you are sugarcoating the pill I am to swallow," said Alatriste. "But please go directly to the second act."

At the reference to a second act, I heard the poet's quiet laugh. We were all remembering what had happened only a few steps from here during the time of the adventure of the two Englishmen. How don Francisco had come to the captain's aid in the course of an ugly scuffle in which steel had flashed like lightning.

"I have some friends, people I am fond of," said don Francisco. "And they want to talk with you."

He had turned around to see whether I was listening to the conversation, and seemed relieved when it appeared that I was taking in the sights of the plaza. I was, however, listening to every word. In that Madrid and that Spain, an alert youth matures quickly, and despite my youth I already suspected that it did no harm to keep my ears open. Just the opposite. In life, danger lies not in not knowing, but in revealing that you do: It is always good to have a sense of the music before the dance begins.

"That has the sound of a potential employ," the captain was saying.

It was a euphemism, of course. Diego Alatriste's line of "employ" tended to take place in dark alleyways, at so much per swordthrust. A slash across the face, slicing off the ear of a creditor or of a bastard dallying with one's wife, a pistol shot at point-blank range, or a handspan of steel in a man's throat—all that was classified and the pay set by scale. In that very plaza, at any given time, there were at least a dozen professionals who were available for such arrangements.

"Yes." The poet nodded, adjusting his eyeglasses. "And well-paid employ, of course."

Diego Alatriste looked long and hard at his companion. I studied the captain's aquiline profile beneath the broad brim of the hat on which the one note of color was a frowsy red plume.

"It is clear that today you are making an effort to annoy me, don Francisco," he said finally. "Do you imply that I would charge for a service done Your Mercy?"

"It is not for me. It is for a father and his two young sons. They have a problem and have sought my advice."

From high atop the lapis lazuli and alabaster fountain, a sculpture of Diana the locals had dubbed Mariblanca, White Mary, looked down upon us as water sang out of the pipes at her feet. The last light was languishing. Rough-looking soldiers and assassins with huge mustaches, broad swords, and a way of standing with their feet planted solidly apart, very "I am dangerous," were clumped in groups in front of the closed doors of the silk and woolen and book shops, or drinking wine at one of the wretched street stalls. The plaza swarmed with blind men, beggars, and whores whose short mantles separated them from decent ladies in full-length cloaks. Some of the soldiers were known to Alatriste. They greeted him from a distance, and he responded distractedly, touching the brim of his hat.

"Are you involved in the matter?" Alatriste asked.

Don Francisco gave an ambiguous shrug. "Only partly. But for reasons you will soon understand, I must see it through to the end."

We kept passing hard-looking men with shifty eyes who sauntered along the iron rails that set off the atrium of the Buen Suceso church. That atrium, and the nearby Calle

Montera, were frequented by men with big talk and large swords. Altercations were common, and entry to the church had been blocked so that after a dispute fugitives could not run into the church for sanctuary. There not even the Law could touch them. They called such escape "safe harboring," or used the euphemisms "going to mass" or "taking a quiet moment of prayer."

"Dangerous?" asked Alatriste.

"Very."

"It will involve swordplay, I imagine."

"I hope not. But there are greater risks than being wounded."

The captain walked on a bit, contemplating in silence the chapel of La Victoria convent that rose behind the houses at the end of the plaza, there at the top of San Jerónimo road. It was not possible to walk around a corner in that city without coming across a church.

"And why me?" he asked finally.

Don Francisco laughed again, quietly, as before.

"'Sblood," he said. "Because you are my friend. And also because try as they may—executioner, court recorder, scribe—you never sing when you are fated to swing, turning lengths of cords into chords."

Thoughtfully, the captain ran his fingers around the neck of his collar. "Well paid, I believe you said."

"That I did."

"By you, Your Mercy?"

"How would you have it? The only way I know to get a fire blazing is to feed it."

Alatriste's hand was still at his throat. "Every time you propose a commission that is well paid, it involves placing my neck in the executioner's noose."

"And that is also true in this case," the poet admitted.

"By the good Christ, that is fine encouragement you offer me."

"It would be deceitful to lie to you."

As he answered, the captain's sarcasm was palpable. "And how is it that you always become involved in such affairs, don Francisco? Only now have you been returned to the king's favor following your long dispute with the Duque de Osuna."

"Therein lies the *quid* of the *quo,* my friend," the poet lamented. "Curse the good nature that leads me into such misadventures. But there are commitments and . . . my honor is at stake."

"And your head, you say."

Now it was don Francisco who looked with mocking amusement at Diego Alatriste. "And also yours, Captain, if you decide to accompany me."

The "if you decide" was superfluous, and both knew it. Even so, the captain's pensive smile lingered on his lips. He looked from side to side, skirted a pile of stinking garbage, distractedly greeted a woman with a scandalously low décolletage who winked at him from a wine shop, and finally threw his hands up.

"And why should I do it? My old *tercio* leaves for Flanders shortly, and I am seriously considering a change of scenery."

"Why should you do it?" Don Francisco stroked his mustache and his goatee. "Well, by my faith, I do not know. Perhaps because when a friend is in difficulty, we have no choice but to fight."

"Fight? A moment ago you were rather confident that there would be no dispute."

The captain had turned to study don Francisco closely. By now the sky over Madrid was growing dark, and the first shadows stretched toward us from the squalid alleyways that led to the plaza. The outlines of objects were beginning to blur, along with the features of passersby. Someone in one of the shops lighted a lantern. Beneath the brim of don Francisco's felt hat, the light reflected from the lenses of his eyeglasses.

"That is true," the poet said. "But should something go wrong, perhaps one element that might not be missing would be a bit of swordplay."

Again he laughed, always in that quiet tone, and with little humor. And at the end, I heard the same laugh from Captain Alatriste. After that, not a word from either. I was in a state of wonderment, knowing I was being led toward new adventures and perils. I followed their dark, hushed silhouettes. Then don Francisco said good-bye, and Captain Alatriste stood alone a moment, motionless and silent in the darkness. I dared not go to him or speak a word. He stood there as if he had forgotten my presence, until the bells in La Victoria tolled nine on the clock.

II. THE NECK AND THE NOOSE

They came the next morning. I heard their footsteps on the creaking staircase that led up from the courtyard, and when I ran to open the door, the captain was already there, in his shirtsleeves and looking very serious. I had observed that during the night he had cleaned his pistols, and that one had been left, oiled and ready, on the table near the beam where his belt with the sword and dagger hung from a nail.

"Go outside for a walk, Íñigo."

I obeyed, but when I went out into the hall I met don Francisco de Quevedo on the top steps. He was accompanied by three caballeros, though he acted as if he didn't know them. I noted that they had not used the door on Calle Arcabuz, but the one between our courtyard and Caridad la Lebrijana's tavern, the entrance on Calle Toledo, which was used less often and was, therefore, more discreet. Don Francisco cuffed me on the cheek affectionately before he went into our rooms, and I continued on along the gallery, but not before I sneaked a quick look at his companions. One was an older man, quite gray. The other two were young, one about eighteen and the other not far into his twenties. Nice-looking youths who bore a certain resemblance to each other; perhaps brothers or close relatives. All three were dressed in traveling clothes, and something about them said "not Madrileños."

I swear to Your Mercies that I was a well-mannered and discreet young lad. I am not a meddler, nor was I then. But to a boy of thirteen, the world is a fascinating spectacle and he wants to taste every morsel. To that we must add the words I had overheard between Señor de Quevedo and Captain Alatriste the evening before. So if I am to be honest, I must confess that I went around the gallery, pulled myself up to the roof with all the agility of my youth, and, after scooting along an eave to a window, cautiously reentered the house. I squatted at the back of a cupboard in my room, where a certain crack allowed me to see and hear everything that was happening on the other side. I was careful not to make a sound, and determined not to miss a single detail of this business in which, according to don Francisco's own words, both Diego Alatriste and he were gambling their lives. What I did not know—God save me!—was how I would come within a hair of losing my own.

"You are aware," the captain was summing up, "that the penalty for breaking into a convent is death."

Don Francisco de Quevedo nodded but said nothing. He had made the introductions and then stepped aside, letting the visitors speak. Of those three, it was the older man who had led the conversation. He was sitting beside the table that held his hat, a jug of wine no one had touched, and the captain's pistol.

"The danger is real," the older man said. "But there is no other way to rescue my daughter."

I later learned that his name was Vicente de la Cruz; he was from an old family in Valencia and only temporarily in Madrid. He was thin, with white hair and beard, and though he must have been over sixty years old, he was vigorous and erect in his gait. His sons, the elder of whom had yet to see twenty-five, looked very much like him. Their names were don Jerónimo and don Luis. The latter was the younger; already very poised, though not more than eighteen. The three men were wearing simple traveling or hunting garb, the father in a black woolen shirt and blue doublet, and his sons in dark green cloth with trim of the same color. Each carried a sword and dagger in an old-fashioned baldric. Their hair was cut very short, and they shared a candid expression that accentuated the family resemblance.

"Who are the priests?" asked Alatriste.

He was leaning against an exposed beam in the wall, his thumbs hooked into his belt, mulling it all over. His eye was more on Señor Quevedo than the visitors, as if asking him what the Devil he had got him into. For his part, the poet, at the window, was staring at the neighboring rooftops as if none of this had anything to do with him. Only from time to time did he send Alatriste a dispassionate glance—very much the bystander—or study his nails with unwonted attention.

"Fray Juan Coroado and Fray Julián Garzo," don Vicente replied. "They own and run the convent, and Sor Josefa, the prioress, speaks only through them. The rest of the nuns either have thrown their lot in with them, or live in fear."

Again Captain Alatriste looked at don Franciso de Quevedo, and this time he caught his eye. *I am sorry*, the poet's silence seemed to say. *You are the only one who can help me.*

"Fray Juan, the chaplain," don Vicente continued, "is the minion of the Conde de Olivares. His father, Amandio

Coroado, founded the convent of the Adoratrices Benitas at his own expense, and is, in addition, the only Portuguese banker the king's favorite can rely on. Now that Olivares is attempting to cease his dealings with the Genoese, Coroado is his ace card for getting money out of Portugal to fund the war in Flanders. For that reason, Fray Juan, his son, enjoys absolute impunity in the convent and outside it."

"These are very serious accusations."

"They have been proved time and again. This Juan Coroada is not some simple, credulous priest, like so many; not one of the Illuminati, not a mere petitioner, not a fanatic. He is thirty years old. He has money, position at court, and he cuts a handsome figure. He is a pervert who has turned the convent into his private seraglio."

"There is a more explicit word, Father," put in the younger of the sons. His voice trembled with anger, and he was almost stuttering; anyone could see that he was restraining himself out of respect for his father.

Don Vicente de la Cruz reprimanded him, frowning. "Perhaps. But as your sister is there, dare not be so bold as to speak it."

The youth paled and bowed his head, as his elder brother, less vocal and more self-possessed, put a hand on his arm.

"And the other priest?" pressed Alatriste.

The light falling through the window illuminated the side of the captain's face, leaving the other side in shadow. It highlighted his scars: the one over the left eyebrow and another, more recent, at the hairline in the center of his brow, a souvenir of the skirmish in the yard of El Príncipe theater. The third visible scar, across the back of his left hand, was also recent and also from a dagger. That had been acquired in the ambush at the Gate of Lost Souls. Unseen, covered by clothing, were four others, the latest being the wound that had mustered him out of the Battle of Fleurus, the one that some nights kept him from sleeping.

"Fray Julián Garzo is the confessor," don Vicente de la Cruz replied. "Another admirable church leader. He has an uncle on the Council of Castile. That renders him untouchable, like his confrere."

"In other words, two men to watch out for."

Don Luis, the younger son, could barely contain himself, his fist squeezing the pommel of his sword. "What you mean is two dogs, two swine."

He was choking on his repressed anger, and that made him seem even younger; that, and the blond, still unshaven, fuzz on his upper lip. His father sent him another frowning glance, demanding silence before he continued.

"The fact is," he said, "that the walls of La Adoración convent are thick enough to silence all that goes on within them: a chaplain who veils his lasciviousness beneath a hypocritical mysticism, a stupid and credulous prioress, and a congregation of unfortunate women who have been convinced that they have celestial visions or are possessed of the Devil." The caballero ran his fingers through his beard as he spoke, and it was obvious that acting with equanimity and decorum was costing him dear. "They are even told that through love for and obedience to the chaplain they may find the way to God, and that certain intimacies and unchaste acts proposed by the spiritual director are the pathway to perfection."

Diego Alatriste was far from being surprised. In the Spain of our very Catholic monarch, Philip IV, faith was usually sincere, but its external manifestations often resulted in hypocrisy in the privileged, and superstition in the common folk. In that broad panorama, many clergy were fanatic and ignorant, a vulgar assemblage of ne'er-do-wells who wanted to escape employment or military service; some, ambitious and immoral, hoped to better their social situation, more devoted to their own good than to the glory of God. While the poor paid taxes from which the rich and the religious by profession were excluded, legal scholars argued whether ecclesiastic immunity was or was not a divine right. And there were many who took advantage of the tonsure to satisfy contemptible appetites and self-interest. The result was that side by side with unquestionably honorable and saintly clerics, one also found the vile and avaricious: priests who had concubines and bastard children, confessors who preyed on women in the confessional, nuns who entertained lovers, convents that were havens for illicit affairs. These scandals that were the daily, if not exactly hallowed, bread.

"No one has condemned what is happening there?"

Don Vicente de la Cruz nodded dejectedly. "Yes. I myself. I even sent a detailed reminder to the Conde de Olivares, the king's right hand, but have no reply."

"And the Inquisition?"

"They are informed. I had a conversation with a member of the Supreme Council. He promised to attend to my request, and I know that he sent two Trinitarian examiners to look into the matter. But between the efforts of Father Coroado and Father Garzo, and the collaboration of the prioress, they were convinced that all was in order, and they left with only good things to say."

"Which is by all accounts strange," interposed don Francisco de Quevedo. "The Inquisition has been keeping a sharp eye on the Conde de Olivares, and this would be a good pretext for harassing him."

The Valencian shrugged. "That is what we believed. But no doubt they decided they would be spending too much good coin to protect a simple novice. Furthermore, Sor Josefa, the prioress, enjoys a reputation at court for being a pious woman. She devotes a daily mass and special prayers to Olivares, and the king and queen, of course, asking God to send them male heirs. That assures her respect and prestige, when in fact, except for a smattering of inconsequential knowledge, she is merely a foolish woman who has been sucked into the whirlpool of the chaplain's charm. The case is not unusual, now that every prioress worth her salt must have at least five stigmata and exude the scent of sanctity."

Don Vicente smiled with bitterness and scorn. "Her mystic aspirations, her desire to be center stage, her dreams of grandeur, and her connections, have led her to believe that she is a new Santa Teresa. In addition, ducats fall like rain from Father Coroado's fingers, making La Adoración the wealthiest convent in Madrid. More than a few families want to place their daughters there."

I was listening through the chink in the wall, not overly shocked despite my youth. In a society in which religion and immorality went hand in hand, confessors were notorious for taking tyrannical possession of the souls, and at times the bodies, of devout women—with scandalous consequences.

As for the influence of those in the religious life, it was immense. Different orders formed enmities and alliances among themselves. Priests forbade their faithful to reconcile with other congregations, and when it was their whim, they blithely severed family ties, even counseled disobedience of authority. Neither was it unusual to see clerics who preyed on women employ a mystic-amatory language that evoked the divine, nor veil prurient passions and appetites, ambition and lust, under the guise of spiritual exercises. The figure of the predatory priest was well known, and widely satirized, in that century, as in these explicit verses from *La cueva de Meliso*.

Inside, you will hear the confessions
of beauteous servants of God.
You may treat them as wives.
They believe they live honorable lives
and that you are purging demonic obsessions.

It was not surprising, in that time of superstition and sanctimoniousness, that such wickedness prevailed, given that we Spaniards lived in so little accord, badly fed, and worse governed amidst collective pessimism and disillusion. Sometimes we sought the consolation of religion because we felt we were on the brink of an abyss, and others for simple, bare-faced, earthly gain.

This situation was aggravated by the numbers of priests and nuns who had no calling for the cloth—there were more than nine thousand convents when I was a boy—the result of the practice of penniless noble families who, unable to wed their daughters with traditional decorum, instead directed them to the religious life, or incarcerated them against their will following some worldly indiscretion. Cloisters were filled with women who did not wish to be nuns. It was they to whom don Luis Hurtado de Toledo—the author, or, to be more accurate, the translator, of *Palmerin of England*—was referring in these famous lines.

> *For our fathers, having commended*
> *our family's fortunes to their sons,*
> *depriving us, have intended*
> *to imprison us in this place where*
> *God is outrageously offended.*

Don Francisco de Quevedo had not moved from his place by the window; he seemed removed from the conversation, staring vacantly at the cats wandering across the roof tiles like idle soldiers. Captain Alatriste gave him a long look before turning back to don Vicente de la Cruz.

"I do not yet understand," he said, "how your daughter came to find herself in this situation."

The elderly man was slow to reply. The same light that accentuated the captain's scars split his brow with a deep vertical furrow that spoke of his profound grief.

"Elvira came to Madrid with two other novices when La Adoración was founded, about a year ago. They were accompanied by a duenna, a woman who had been highly recommended to us, who was to wait upon them until they took their vows."

"And what does this duenna say?"

The captain's question was met with a silence thick enough to be sliced with a scimitar. Don Vicente de la Cruz was staring at his bony, gnarled, but still strong right hand where it rested on the table. His sons were scowling at the floor as if studying something in front of their boots. I had observed that don Jerónimo, the elder son, rougher and more taciturn than his brother, had a hard, piercing gaze that I had seen in only a few men, something I was learning to take as warning. The look of a man who while others strut about clanking their swords against the furniture and boasting in loud voices, sits quietly in a corner of the gaming house, unblinking, taking in every detail, not opening his mouth, until suddenly he gets up and without changing expression walks over and skewers you with a sword. Captain Alatriste himself was such a man; and I, from being so long near him, was beginning to recognize the type.

"We do not know what has become of the duenna," don Vicente said finally. "She disappeared a few days ago."

Again that silence. This time don Francisco de Quevedo took his gaze from the roof tiles and the cats. His deeply melancholy eyes met those of Diego Alatriste.

"Disappeared," the captain repeated, as if turning the words over in his mind.

Don Vicente de la Cruz's sons were still examining the floor. Finally the father abruptly nodded. It seemed he could not take his eyes from the motionless hand on the table beside the hat, the jug of wine, and the captain's pistol.

"Yes," he said. "She cannot be found."

Don Francisco de Quevedo moved away from the window and took a few steps into the room, stopping beside Alatriste. "They say," he murmured, "that she served as a go-between for Fray Juan Coroado."

"And she has disappeared."

For a few instants the captain and don Francisco stood toe to toe.

"So we have heard," the poet finally affirmed.

"I understand."

Even I, in my hiding place, understood, though I didn't yet comprehend exactly what role don Francisco was playing in such a scabrous affair. As for the rest of it, perhaps the pouch that Martín Saldaña had found in the possession of the strangled woman in the sedan chair, could not, after all, buy enough masses to save her soul.

Wide-eyed, I peered through the chink in the cupboard, beginning to feel more respect for don Vicente de la Cruz and his sons. He did not seem as aged now, or his sons as young. After all, I thought, shuddering, it was their sister and daughter who was involved. I had sisters of my own back in Oñate, and I do not know how far I might go to avenge them.

"Now," the father continued, "the prioress says that Elvira has turned her back on the world forever. We have not been able to visit her for eight months."

"Why has she not run away?"

Don Vicente made a helpless gesture. "She is under their sway in what happens to her. The nuns and the novices spy on one another. Imagine the scene: visions and exorcisms, confessions used to practice unholy ceremonies behind closed doors, under the pretext of cleansing the nuns of devils, jealousy, envy—all their petty convent quarrels." The Valencian's stoic expression crumpled into a picture of pain. "Nearly all the sisters are very young, like Elvira. Any who do not believe they are possessed of a demon, or have celestial visions, invent them to attract attention. The stupid prioress, who has no will of her own, is in the hands of the chaplain, whom she considers a saint. And Fray Juan and his acolyte roam from cell to cell giving solace and comfort."

"Have you, Your Mercy, spoken with the chaplain?"

"Once. And I swear on the life of our king that had we not been in the locutory of the convent I would have killed him on the spot." Don Vicente de la Cruz held up his inert right hand, incensed, as if he lamented that it was not bathed in blood.

"Despite my gray hairs, he laughed in my face with unbearable insolence. Because our family . . ."

He stopped mid-sentence and looked at his sons. The younger was deathly pale, without a drop of color in his face, and his brother was looking away with that frightening expression of his.

"In truth," their father continued, "the purity of our blood is not categorical. My great-grandfather was a convert to the Faith, and my grandfather was harassed by the Inquisition. All that took a great deal of money to resolve. That swine, Padre Coroado, knew how to play that card. He threatened to denounce my daughter for having Jewish blood . . . and us as well."

"Which is not true," the younger son intervened. "Although we have the misfortune of not being old Christians, our family is without blemish. The proof of that is that don Pedro Téllez, the Duque de Osuna, honored my father with his confidence when he served under him in Sicily."

He stopped suddenly; his pallor changed to pomegranate red. I watched Captain Alatriste look at don Francisco: now the connection was clear. During his reign as Viceroy of Sicily, and later Naples, the Duque de Osuna had been Quevedo's friend, and Quevedo, too, had suffered during Osuna's fall from favor. It was obvious that the obligation that bound the poet to don Vicente de la Cruz was to be found in that tangle of relationships, and that the Valencian's misfortune and abandonment at court was mud stirred from that dust. In addition, don Francisco knew how it was to find oneself abandoned by people who in other times had sought one's favors and influence.

"What is the plan?" the captain asked.

I heard in his voice a tone I knew very well: resignation, and an absence of illusions concerning the chances for success or failure. An exhausted, silent resolve, stripped of any concerns other than technical details, the veteran soldier matter-of-factly preparing to confront a bad assignment that was part of his job. Often, in the years ahead, when we were to share adventures and fight in the wars of our lord and king, I recognized that same tone and that unemotional expression that so uniquely hardened the gray-green eyes of the captain after the long immobility of waiting during a campaign, when the drums sounded and the *tercios* marched toward the enemy at that awesome, stately pace beneath the tattered flags that had led us to both glory and disaster. That same look, and that same tone of infinite weariness, became mine many years later: the day when I stood among the remnants of a Spanish formation, dagger between my teeth, pistol in one hand and unsheathed sword in the other. There, I watched the French cavalry form their last charge, as in Flanders, rosy with blood, a sun went down . . . one that for two centuries had inspired fear and respect throughout the world.

But that morning in Madrid, in '23, Rocroi existed only in the dark pages of Destiny, and two decades would pass before that fateful encounter. Our king was young and gallant, Madrid was the capital of two worlds, the old and the new, and I myself was a beardless youth. I crouched impatiently at the crack in a cupboard, waiting for the answer to the question the captain had posed: What plan had don Vicente de la Cruz and his sons, through the good offices of don Francisco de Quevedo, come to present? As the grieving father prepared to answer, a cat jumped through the window and slipped between my legs. I tried, quietly, to brush it away, but it refused to leave. Then I moved too brusquely, and a broom and a tin dust bin crashed to the floor. And when I looked up, horrified, the door had been flung open and the elder son of don Vicente de la Cruz was standing before me, dagger in hand.

.   .   .

"I believed you to be inflexible in regard to purity of blood, don Francisco," said Captain Alatriste, when we three were alone. "I never imagined that you would place your neck in a noose for a family of Jew-turned-Christian *conversos*."

I glimpsed a smile of affectionate indulgence beneath the captain's mustache. Seated at our table, wearing the face of a man with few friends, Señor de Quevedo was dispatching the jug of wine that until that moment no one had touched. After reaching an accord with the captain, don Vicente de la Cruz and his sons had left.

"Everything has its . . . charm," the poet murmured.

"I have no doubt. But if your much-loved Luis de Góngora catches scent of this, you should prepare to be lambasted. His sonnet will drop you to your knees."

"A pox on him."

But it was true. In a time when hatred of Jews and heretics was considered an indispensable component of faith—only a few years earlier, the aforementioned Lope, as well as good don Miguel de Cervantes, had crowed over the expulsion of the Moors—don Francisco de Quevedo, who prided himself on being an old Christian from Santander, was not exactly noted for his tolerance of anyone whose purity of blood was dubious. On the contrary, he often used that theme when aiming darts at his adversaries—and especially don Luis de Góngora, to whom he attributed Jewish blood.

Why should Greek be a tongue you debase?
and not Hebrew? We know you master that,
it is as clear as the nose on your face.

The great satirist liked to intersperse such compliments with allusions to Góngora's sodomy, as he did in a certain famous sonnet that concludes,

Your legs are worse than my poor two.
I limp, it's true, but they do not go
the places your third leg leads you to.

Yet here he was, getting his own hands dirty: don Francisco Gómez de Quevedo y Villegas, he of the habit of Santiago and proven family purity, lord of la Torre de Juan Abad, scourge of Judaizers, heretics, sodomites, and assorted Latinate court poets, risking life and honor, plotting nothing less than to violate the sanctity of a cloister in order to aid a family of Valencian *conversos*. Even I, at my tender age, recognized the terrible implications.

"A pox on him, by Christ," the poet repeated.

I suppose that any sane man would be swearing—in Greek, even Hebrew, both languages that don Francisco was familiar with—had he found himself in Quevedo's starched white collar. And Captain Alatriste, who was not in Quevedo's gorget, but faced ruin enough in his own, was well aware of that.

The captain had not moved from his place against the wall throughout the conversation with our visitors, and his thumbs were still hooked over his belt. He had not shifted position even when Jerónimo de la Cruz returned to the room, dagger in hand, leading me by the ear. Alatriste merely ordered the man to release me, in a tone that inspired my captor, after only an instant's hesitation, to obey. As for me, the awkward moment past, I was huddled in a corner, still red with embarrassment, trying to pass unnoticed. It had taken a certain effort to convince the father and sons that although disobedient, I was a prudent lad and could be trusted. Don Francisco himself had to speak for me. But the beans had been spilled—I had heard everything—and don Vicente de la Cruz and his sons would have to put their faith in me. Although when it came down to it—as the captain clarified very deliberately, casting cold, intimidating looks at each of the three in turn—this was no longer a situation in which they could offer an opinion or have a choice. That declaration was followed by a long and weighty silence, after which my involvement was not questioned again.

"They are good people," Quevedo said finally. "And blood or no blood, no one can accuse them of not being good Catholics." He paused in search of further justification. "And when we were in Italy, don Vicente performed a number of services for me. It would have been wicked not to hold out a hand to him."

Captain Alatriste nodded his understanding, and beneath his military mustache I could see the same irrepressible smile.

"All that you say is well and good," the captain acknowledged. "But I press my point about Góngora. After all, Your Mercy is constantly dwelling on his Semitic nose and his aversion to the flesh of the pig. You remember when you wrote,

"No white shows in your hair,
so old Christian you cannot be:
sonofa something, no question there,
but son of pure blood? A mockery."

Don Francisco smoothed his mustache and goatee, half pleased that the captain remembered his verses, and half annoyed by the bantering way he recited them.

"By the good Christ, Alatriste, what a good—and, I might add, badly timed—memory you have."

Alatriste burst out laughing, unable to contain himself any longer, which did not improve the poet's humor.

"I can just imagine what your enemy will write," said the captain, beating a dead horse, holding his fingers as if he were writing on air.

"You say, don Francisco, I am a filthy Jewish pig,
while you dance to the tune of a lively Hebrew jig . . .

"What do you think?"

Don Franciso's face grew even more dour. Were it not Diego Alatriste speaking, his tormentor would have tasted steel some time ago.

"Bad, and with very little flair," was all he said, dispiritedly. "Those lines could, in fact, have been written by that Cordovan sodomite, or that other friend of yours, the Conde de Guadalmedina, whose behavior as a caballero I do not contest, but who as a poet is the mortification of Parnassus. As for Góngora, that puerile asshole, that proparoxytonic, euphistic versifier, that dabbler in vortices, tricliniums, promptuaria, and vacillating Icaruses, that shadow on the sun and eructation of the wind . . . he is the last thing that worries me now. I do fear, however, that I have brought you into a bad business." He gripped the jug of wine more tightly and took another swig, glancing in my direction. "And the lad."

The lad—that is, I—was still in the corner. The cat

had strolled past me three times, and I had made every effort to get in a good kick, with little success. I saw that Alatriste, too, was looking at me, and he was no longer smiling.
Finally he shrugged his shoulders.

"The *lad* got himself into it," he declared calmly. "As
for me, do not concern yourself." He pointed to the pouch
of gold *escudos* in the center of the table. "They have paid,
and that eases all cares."

"Perhaps."

The poet did not seem convinced, and Alatriste's lips
again twisted with irony.

"What the devil, don Francisco. It is a little late for
regrets, now that you've already got me dressed for the ball."

Dejected, the poet took a swallow, and then another.
His eyes had begun to water.

"But to turn a convent upside down," he said, under-
scoring the obvious, "is not a trifling matter."

"Nor is taking La Goleta, *pardiez!*" The captain strode
to the table, where he picked up his pistol and removed
the primer and charge. "They tell that my mother's great-
uncle, a man well known in the day of Charles the Fifth,
broke into a convent one day in Seville."

Don Francisco looked up, interested. "Was he one who
inspired Tirso's play?"

"So they say."

"I was not aware that you were related."

"Well, now you know it. Spain is a pocket handker-chief: here everyone knows everyone, and all roads cross."

Quevedo's eyeglasses were dangling from their cord. Thoughtful, he held them a moment but did not place them on his nose. Instead, they dropped from his fingers to again hang above the embroidered cross on his chest, and he reached instead for the wine. He drank a long, last draught, gazing lugubriously at the captain over the lip of the jug.

"Well, by the good Christ, I venture that your uncle, that trickster Don Juan, had a bad third act."

III. MADRID STEEL

The next morning found me at mass with Diego Alatriste and Señor de Quevedo, a rather momentous event. Don Francisco, both because of his Santander heritage and his cross of Santiago, felt it a point of honor to fulfill the rituals of the Church, but the captain was not moved a hair by a *Dominus* or a *vobiscum*. It is, however, only fair to point out that for all his oaths, moderate in themselves, for all the blasphemy and By Gods, only standard in his former profession, never in all the years I spent at his side did I hear Alatriste speak a word against religion. Not even when, in the Tavern of the Turk, his friends' controversial comments left Dómine Pérez in the middle and no maxim with a breath of life. Alatriste did not practice Catholicism but he respected tonsures, robes, and wimples in the same way that he respected the authority and the person of our lord and king. Perhaps it was his discipline as a soldier, or it may have been the stoic indifference that seemed to govern his moods and his character. A further detail: though he so seldom attended mass himself, the captain always obliged me to pay my dues to God every Sunday and feast day, whether in the company of Caridad la Lebrijana— like all former whores, La Lebrijana was extremely pious— or Dómine Pérez. And two days a week, at Alatriste's insistence, the good priest taught me grammar, a little Latin, and enough catechism and Sacred History that, as the captain said, no one would take me for a Turk or an accursed heretic.

He was a man of many contradictions. Not much later, in Flanders, I had occasion to see him kneeling with bowed head as the *tercios* were preparing for combat and the chaplains were going up and down the rows blessing all the men. He did not do it to affect piety but, rather, to show respect for comrades who were going off to die believing in the efficacy of the whole rigmarole. Alatriste's God was neither placated by laud nor offended by oaths; He was a powerful and dispassionate being who did not manipulate the puppets on the stage of life, but merely observed them. And it was also He who, with reasons incomprehensible to the actors in the human comedy—why not just call it a farce—operated the stage machinery, causing lethal trapdoors to open or revolving panels to shift suddenly, sometimes imprisoning you in shackles and other times—a literal *deus ex machina*—extracting you from the most dire situations. It might all be due to that long-ago prime motion and efficient cause that Dómine Pérez mentioned one fine afternoon when he had been a bit too free with the sweet wine and was attempting to explain Saint Thomas's five proofs to us. But as for the captain, his interpretation of the matter was possibly closer to what the Romans—if I am not deceived by the Latin I learned from that same *dómine*—called *fatum.*

I remember a taciturn Alatriste, when enemy artillery was creating significant lacunae in our ranks, and all around, fellow soldiers were making the sign of the cross, commending themselves to Christ and the most blessed Virgin. Suddenly you heard them reciting prayers they had learned as children, and the captain murmuring "Amen" along with them, so they would not feel alone when they fell to the ground and died. His cold, gray-green eyes nevertheless were fixed on the undulating rows of the enemy cavalry, on the musket fire issuing from the terreplein of a dike, on the smoking bombs that snaked across the ground before exploding in a burst that left the Devil well supplied. It was evident that "Amen" did not bind him in any way, as one could read in the absorbed gaze of an old soldier attentive only to the monotonous drumroll from the center of the *tercio,* a beat as slow and calm as the tranquil pace of the Spanish infantry and the serene beating of his heart. Because Captain Alatriste served God as he served his king. He had no reason to love God, even to admire Him, but being who he was, he afforded the deity his respect.

One day when we had taken a bellyful of steel and shot on the banks of the Merck River, near Breda, I saw Alatriste do battle for a flag and the corpse of our field marshal. And I know that although he was willing to sacrifice his hide—and for good measure mine—for that dead body sieved by musket balls, he did not give a fig for either don Pedro de la Daga *or* the flag. That was what was puzzling about the captain: he could show respect for a God who did not matter to him, fight for a cause in which he did not believe, get drunk with an enemy, or die for an officer or a king he scorned.

Yes, we went to mass, although the motive was far from pious. The church, as Your Mercies will undoubtedly have suspected, was the one attached to the convent of La Adoración. Las Benitas was near the palace and almost straight across from the convent of La Encarnación, which was next to the small plaza of the same name. Las Benitas's eight-o'clock mass was in vogue, for that was where Teresa de

Guzmán, the wife of the Conde de Olivares, came to worship. Furthermore, the chaplain, don Juan Coroado, had a reputation for cutting a fine figure before the altar and preaching a fine homily from the pulpit. So the church was frequented not only by truly religious women but also by ladies of good breeding, drawn there by the Condesa de Olivares or by the chaplain, and by other women who had no breeding at all, but pretended to. Even harlots and flamboyant actresses—as pious in matters of dogma as the next—dropped in with the required devotion, thickly powdered and rouged beneath the folds of their mantillas and fine black silks, and dripping with laces from Lorraine and Provence—those from Flanders being reserved for ladies of greater substance. And since the presence of so many ladies, genteel or otherwise, drew more males than lice to a muleteer's doublet, the famed eight-o'clock mass filled the small church from altar to atrium. Some female worshipers had eyes only for God, while others sent volleys of Cupid's darts flying above their fans. Gallants lurked behind columns or beside the font to offer the ladies holy water; beggars sat on the steps outside the door, exhibiting their sores and pustules and the mutilations supposedly earned in Flanders, even Lepanto, and wrangling over the best places at the exit from the mass, ready to berate arrogantly, as their right, the caballeros and damas who gave themselves airs but would not allow a wretched copper coin to see the light of day.

The three of us positioned ourselves near the door, at a spot from which we could survey both the nave of the church and the choir, and the iron lattice that divided the church from the convent. At that moment, the nave was so jammed with people that had there been only one or two more, the Christ on the main altar would have had to be portrayed hanged, arms at his side, rather than crucified. I watched the captain, hat in hand and cape over his arm, study the plan of the building, just as, when we reached the church, his alert eyes had registered every detail of the garden walls and the façade of the convent. The mass had progressed to the liturgy of the word, and when the celebrant turned to the assembly I was at last able to see the face of the renowned chaplain Coroado, who was reeling off Latin with eloquence, finesse, and aplomb. He seemed to be well favored, elegant beneath the chasuble, thick black hair tonsured and trimmed at the nape of his neck. His eyes were dark and penetrating, and it was not difficult to imagine their effect upon the daughters of Eve, especially in the case of nuns whose order closed off all contact with the world and the opposite sex.

I was incapable of looking at the man without thinking of everything I knew about him, and about the convent in which he made a dressing gown of his cassock. I must apol-

ogize for mentioning the ill feeling and indignation caused
by his ritualized performance, the fatuous unction with
which he celebrated Christ's sacrifice. I was astounded
that no one among the assembly shouted out "sacrilege,"
or "hypocrite," and that I saw nothing around me but devotion, even admiration, in the eyes of many women. But
that is the way of life, and that was but one of the first
times, among no few to come, that I was taught a useful
lesson about how appearances trump truth, and how vil-
lains hide their vices behind masks of piety, honor, and de-
cency. And that to denounce evildoers without proof, attack
them without weapons, trust blindly in reason or justice, is
often the fastest road toward one's own perdition, while
the scoundrels who use influence or money as a shield remain untouched. Another lesson that I learned early on is
that it is a grave error to align our fortunes with those of
the powerful, for we are more certain to lose than to win.
Better to wait, not rush or flounder about, until time or
chance brings the adversary within range of our blade:
something that in Spain—here, sooner or later, we all go
up and come down the same stairway—is normal, even inevitable and expected. And if not, patience. After all, God
has the last word; He shuffles all the cards.

"Second chapel on the left," whispered don Francisco.
"Behind the grille."

Captain Alatriste, whose eyes were focused on the altar,

stood riveted a moment longer, then turned to look in the direction the poet indicated. I followed his gaze toward the chapel that connected the church with the convent, where the black-and-white headdresses of nuns and novices could be glimpsed through the heavy iron lattice, to which, apparently, because of the severity of the cloister rules, spikes had been added to keep any man from approaching too closely. That was our Spain: severe rigor and ceremony, all intimidating spikes, divisive grilles, and grand façades. In the midst of the disasters in Europe, the Cortes of Castile were arguing the dogma of the Immaculate Conception, while predatory priests, nuns without calling, officials, judges, nobles—every mother's son—were quietly raking in fortunes. Indeed, the nation that was mistress of two worlds was becoming the courtyard of the master thief Monipodio, providing an opportunity for larceny and envy and a paradise for go-betweens and Pharisees, all patched together with honors, bought consciences, widespread hunger, and unrestrained wickedness to ease it along.

"What do you think, Captain?"

The poet had spoken very quietly, taking advantage of the moment the parishioners were reciting the profession of faith. In one hand he held his hat, and the other hand was on the pommel of his sword; he was staring straight ahead with a deceptively abstracted air, as if he had nothing but the liturgy on his mind.

"Difficult," Alatriste replied.

The poet's deep sigh blended into the *Deum de Deo, lumen de lumine, Deum verum de Deo vero,* which the communicants were praying in chorus. A little farther away, in the shelter of a column, attempting to pass as unobserved among the crowd as a thief in a circle of scribes, I saw the elder son of don Vicente de la Cruz, the one who had discovered me when the traitorous cat startled me in my hiding place. His face was partially muffled and he was staring toward the nuns' chapel. I wondered whether Elvira de la Cruz was there, and if she could see her brother. The natural romanticism of a youth of my years shot off after the image of that young girl I had never met, but whom I imagined to be a beautiful, tormented prisoner awaiting liberation. The hours in her cell must have become interminable, waiting for a signal, a message, a note announcing that she should be ready to escape. Spurred by my imagination, which flowed so freely at moments that it made me feel like a hero in a book of chivalry—after all, fate *had* made me a part of this enterprise—I squinted hard, trying to pick out Elvira behind the iron latticework that shut her off from the world, and after a moment I saw white fingertips rest for an instant between the heavy bars. I stood there a long time, enchanted, openmouthed, hoping to see the hand appear again, until a well-disguised pinch on the nape of my neck snapped me out of my reverie. Then, against my will, I turned and looked straight ahead, as discreet as anyone could wish. And when the celebrant turned toward us to say *"Dominus vobiscum,"* I looked at his hypocritical face, and without blinking responded, *"Et cum spiritu tuo,"* with such devotion and piety that had my poor old mother seen and heard me, she would have rejoiced.

We left with the *Ite, missa est.* A splendid sun was shining, heightening the colors of the geranium and caraway plants at the windows of La Encarnación across the street. Don Francisco lagged behind, for he knew everyone in Madrid— he had as many friends as enemies—and was enjoying flirting with some of the ladies and conversing with their companions, peering between them from time to time to catch a glimpse of the captain and me as we strolled alongside the wall of Las Benitas's garden. I noticed that the captain was paying special attention to a small door, locked from inside, in the brick wall that was ten feet tall at that point. He also took note of a carriage guard at the corner that would make it possible for someone with sufficient agility to leap over the top. I watched as his keen eyes studied the little door as if he were searching for breaches in an enemy wall. I knew he was interested because he was making that gesture so typical of him: stroking his mustache with two fingers, a sign that usually—reflectively or angrily—preceded putting a hand to his sword when someone was beginning to try his patience. It was at this juncture that the elder son of don Vicente de la Cruz, his hat pulled low on his forehead, caught up with us, though he gave no sign of recognizing us. I observed, however, by the way he was walking and guardedly looking around, that he too was inspecting Las Benitas's walls.

At that moment a small incident occurred that I relate here because it is a good example of Diego Alatriste's nature. We had paused a moment as the captain pretended to be adjusting his belt in order to examine the lock of the door, when we were overtaken by a foursome leaving mass: a pair of foppish young men accompanying two rather common, but beautiful, women. One of the men, the one wearing a velvet doublet with slashed sleeves, a multitude of ribbons and bows, and a silver-embroidered band around the crown of his hat, bumped into me and then, ill-humoredly, shoved me aside, calling me a little pissant. I was not as yet carrying a dagger, because of my youth, but a few years later that discourtesy would have cost him, however well dressed he might be, a stab in the groin with the dagger. Soon, in Flanders, I would carry one as if I'd never been without it.

But at that time I still had no choice but to eat insults without seasoning and without recourse, unless Captain Alatriste determined to take my defense upon himself. Which is precisely what he did, and I must tell you that his actions led me to consider that, despite his often surly ways and silences, the captain held me in esteem. And if Your Mercies will forgive me, I will say that he had good reason, *pardiez*, considering certain pistol shots I had fired on his behalf some time ago at the Gate of Lost Souls.

The fact is that when he heard this dandy debase me, the captain turned, slowly, serenely. On his face was the look of glacial calm that those who know him consider fair notice that it is advisable to take three steps back.

"By God, Íñigo"—the captain seemed to be speaking to me, although he was staring hard at the offender—"I do believe that this caballero has confused you with some rogue of his acquaintance."

I said nothing, not a word, for it was obvious what was happening. The coxcomb, hearing himself addressed, had stopped, and his companions with him. He was the kind of man who uses his own shadow as a kind of mirror. At the captain's "By God," he had placed a white hand displaying a large gold and diamond ring upon the guard of his sword, and with the evident sarcasm of that "caballero," his fingers drummed a tune on the pommel. His arrogant eyes looked Diego Alatriste up and down. When he had completed the inspection, however—after noting the captain's sword with the guard scratched and nicked from other blades, the battle scars on his face, the cold eyes beneath the broad-brimmed hat—the arrogance was not quite as noticeable as it had been.

Even so, he replied. "And what happens," he said disagreeably, "if I am *not* confused and if I *am* certain of what I say . . . eh?"

His answer had sounded firm, which was in the man's favor, although that final hesitation had not escaped me, nor the swift glances he threw toward his companion and the two ladies. In those days, a man might well let himself be killed for the sake of his reputation, and the only things that could not be forgiven were cowardice and dishonor. After all, honor was supposed to be the exclusive patrimony of the hidalgo; and the hidalgo, unlike the plebeian who bore all the tributes and taxes, neither worked nor contributed to the royal treasury. The famous plays of Lope, Tirso, and Calderón often made reference to the chivalric tradition of earlier centuries, but what actually set the tone of the society was the prevalence of scoundrels and swindlers of every stripe. Those hyperboles of honor and dishonor glossed over the business—quite serious, of course—of living without working or paying taxes.

Very slowly, taking his time, the captain ran two fingers over his mustache. And then, with the same hand, without ostentation or exaggeration, he pulled back his cape, further exposing, in addition to his sword, the dagger he wore over his kidney, on the left side.

"What happens," Alatriste replied in measured tones, "if you are not confused? Well, perhaps Your Mercies may find the troublemaker whom I am sure you have mistaken for this lad, if you will come along with me to the de la Vega gate."

The de la Vega gate, which was not far away, was one of the places on the outskirts of the city where men went to resolve their quarrels. And the gesture of freeing up, without further preamble, the Toledo and Biscay weapons had not gone unnoticed by anyone present. Nor had the plural, "Your Mercies," which brought his companion into the game.

The women raised their eyebrows, intrigued, for their gender was a guarantee of safe conduct, allowing them to be privileged spectators. For his part, the second individual— another popinjay distinguished by his goatee, large lace collar, and suede gloves—who had witnessed the prologue with a superior smile, suddenly stopped smiling. It was one thing to go for a stroll with a friend and to bluster a bit before the two ladies, but it was a far different matter to find oneself in a confrontation with a fellow who had the look of a soldier and who, out of the blue, was suggesting they bypass formalities and settle the business immediately with their swords. The companion's expression said, *This is not one of those all-for-show braggarts you see on Calle Montera,* and he communicated this thought further by quietly moving back a few steps. As for the pretty-boy himself, his pallor betrayed that he was thinking exactly the same thing, although his position was more delicate. He had spoken a little too freely, and the problem with words is that once spoken, they cannot find their way back to the speaker alone. Sometimes they have to be returned on the tip of a sword.

"The boy was not to blame," said the companion.

He had spoken like an hidalgo, voice firm and calm, but conciliation was evident in his words. He wanted to remove himself from the center of things and in addition provide his friend with a way out, giving him a foothold whereby he could end the incident without his doublet slashed as generously as his sleeves.

I saw the dandy uncurl the fingers of his right hand and then close them again. He hesitated. Things could be worse. By pure arithmetic, it was two against one, and had he discovered the least sign of discomfort or emotion in Diego Alatriste he might have gone forward—on de la

Vega hill, or right there. But there was something about
the captain's cool demeanor, an indifference so absolute that
it transcended his immobility and his silences that counseled "proceed with great caution." I knew exactly what
was going through his head: a man who challenges a pair
of well-armed strangers either is very sure of himself and
his sword, or he is mad. And neither of the two possibilities was to be treated lightly. Even so, I have to say that the
caballero was not fainthearted. He did not want to fight,
but neither did he want to lose face; so for a few instants
more he locked eyes with the captain. Then he looked
toward me, as if seeing me for the first time.

"I agree that the boy was not to blame," he said finally.

The women smiled, though not without a little disap-
pointment at being deprived of entertainment. The friend
contained a sigh of relief. As for me, it did not matter
whether the pretty-boy apologized or not. I was attuned to
Captain Alatriste's profile beneath the brim of his hat, his
thick mustache, his chin, badly shaved that morning, his
scars, the gray-green, expressionless eyes that had looked
into a void only he could contemplate. Then I looked at his
worn and mended doublet, the ancient cape, the modest
collar washed time and time again by Caridad la Lebrijana, the dull reflection of the sun on the sword guard and
dagger grip protruding from his belt. And I was conscious
of a dual and magnificent privilege: that man had been

my father's friend, and now he was also mine, ready to fight on my behalf over a mere word.

Or maybe, in truth, he was doing it for himself. Perhaps the king's wars, the patrons who hired his sword, the friends who embroiled him in dangerous undertakings, the loose-tongued fops and dandies, even I myself, were simply pretexts that allowed Alatriste to fight because—as don Francisco de Quevedo would have said—there was no choice *but* to fight, regardless of God, and against whatever there was to be against. And don Francisco himself was now hurrying to join us, sniffing a conflict, though a bit late.

I would have followed Captain Alatriste to the Gates of Hell at one word, one gesture, one smile. I was far from suspecting that that was precisely where he was leading me.

I believe I have already spoken of Angélica de Alquézar. Over the years, when I was a soldier like Diego Alatriste—and played other roles that will be told in good time—life placed women in my path. I am not given to the bluff and bluster of the tavern, nor to lyrical nostalgia, but since the tale demands some comment, I shall boil the matter down and state that I loved a certain number of them, and that I recall others with tenderness, indifference, or—most often the case—with a happy and complicit smile. That is the highest laurel a man may hope for, to emerge from such sweet embraces unscathed, with his purse little diminished, his health reasonable, and his esteem intact.

That being said, I shall affirm to Your Mercies that of all the women whose paths crossed mine, the niece of the royal secretary, Luis de Alquézar, was without doubt the most beautiful, the most intelligent, the most seductive, and the most evil. You will make the objection, perhaps, that my youth may have made me excessively vulnerable— remember that at the time of this story I was a lad from the Basque country, not yet fourteen, who had been in Madrid no more than a year. But that was not the case. Even later, when I was a man grown and Angélica was in the full bloom of her womanhood, my sentiments were unchanged. It was like loving the Devil, even knowing who he is.

I believe that I have recounted previously that youthful or not, I was obsessively in love with that señorita. Mine was not yet the passion that comes with years and time, when flesh and blood are blended with dreams, and everything takes on a diffuse and dangerous tone. At the time I am referring to, mine was a kind of hypnotic attraction, like peering into an abyss that tempts you and terrifies you at the same time. Only later—the adventure of the convent and of the dead woman was merely a station on that

Via Crucis—I learned how misleading the blond curls and blue eyes of that angelic-looking girl could be, the cause of my so often finding myself on the verge of sacrificing my honor and my life. In spite of everything, however, I went on loving her to the end. And even now when Angélica de Alquézar and the others are gone, familiar ghosts in my memory, I swear to God above and to all the demons of Hell—where she is most surely a bright flame today—that I love her still. At times, when memories seem so sweet that I long even for old enemies, I go and stand before the portrait Diego Velázquez painted of her, and stay for hours looking at her in silence, painfully aware that I never truly knew her. But along with the scars that she inflicted, my old heart still holds the conviction that that girl, that woman who inflicted upon me every evil she was capable of, also, in her way, loved me till the day she died.

At the time of this story, however, all that lay before me. The morning that I followed her carriage to the Acero fountain, beyond the Manzanares and the Segovia bridge, Angélica de Alquézar was simply a fascinating enigma. I have already written that she used to ride down Calle Toledo on the way between her domicile and the palace, where she served as a *menina*, waiting upon the queen and the princesses. The house where she lived, an old mansion on the corner of La Encomienda and Los Embajadores, belonged

to her uncle, Luis de Alquézar. It had been the property of
the Marqués de Ortígolas until he—ruined by a well-known
actress in La Cruz theater, who choked more life out of
him than a hangman his victims—had to sell it to satisfy
his creditors. Luis de Alquézar had never married, and his
one known weakness, aside from the voracious exercise of
power that had earned him his position at court, was his
orphaned niece, the daughter of a sister who had perished
with her husband, a duke, during the storm that lashed
the fleet of the Indies in '21.

I had watched her pass by, as was my habit, from my post
at the door of the Tavern of the Turk. Sometimes I followed
her two-mule carriage to the Plaza Mayor, or sometimes to
the very flagstones of the palace, where I turned and followed my footsteps home. All for the fleeting reward of
one of her disturbingly blue glances—which on occasion
she deigned to grant me before focusing on some detail of
the landscape, or turning toward the duenna who usually
accompanied her: a hypocritical, vinegary old woman as
worn and thin as a student's purse. The duenna was one of
those creatures of whom it could honestly be said,

Never without her scapular,
with more herbs and balms and flummery
than all the nostrums that line the shelves
of the city's most bustling pharmacy.

I had, as you perhaps recall, exchanged a few words with Angélica during the adventure of the two Englishmen, and I always suspected that, knowingly or not, she had contributed to our being attacked in El Príncipe theater, where Captain Alatriste came within a hair of losing his hide. But no one is completely in control of whom he hates or whom he loves; so, even knowing that, the blonde girl continued to bewitch me. And my intuition that it was all a devilishly dangerous game did nothing but spur my imagination.

So I followed her that morning through the Guadalajara gate and de la Villa plaza. It was a brilliant day, but instead of continuing toward the palace, her carriage rolled down the de la Vega hill onto the Segovia bridge and across the river whose thin trickle was the eternal source of burlesque and ridicule from the city's poets. Even the usually cultured and exquisite don Luis de Góngora—quoted here with an apology to Señor de Quevedo—contributed the pretty lines that follow.

An ass drank you in yesterday,
and today you are the piss it passed.

I learned later that Angélica had during that time fallen quite pale, and her physician had recommended outings among the groves and promenades near El Duque garden and the Casa de Campo. He'd also prescribed the renowned waters of the Acero fountain, widely believed to cure, among other things, ladies suffering from amenorrhea, or interruption of various delicate female functions. A fountain described by Lope in one of his plays:

> *Take a walk tomorrow,*
> *if you can endure*
> *a good half-dipper of*
> *Acero-laced water,*
> *the miraculous unblocking cure.*

Angélica was still very young for that type of problem, but it is true that the cool shade there, the sun and the healing air, were good for her. So that was where she was heading, with carriage, coachman, and duenna, and me following some distance behind. On the other side of the bridge and the river, damas and caballeros were strolling beneath the arching trees. In the Madrid of that day, just as I mentioned in regard to the church of Las Benitas, wherever there were ladies—and the Acero fountain attracted not a few, with or without duennas—there also boiled a pot full of gallants, procurers, amorous rendezvous, and other encounters, any of which, fueled by jealousy, might lead to an exchange of words and insults, drawn swords, and a *paseo* ended with swordplay. In that hypocritical

Spain, always a slave to appearances and "What will people say?" where the honor of fathers and husbands was measured by the chastity of their wives and daughters—to the point of not letting them leave the house—activities that were in principle innocent, such as taking the waters or going to mass, engendered a muddle of adventures, intrigues, and liaisons.

I am pretending, my beloved husband,
to be needing "regulation,"
that I may deceive a jealous father
and an aunt's intimidation.

So I apologize to Your Mercies for the youthful spirit of chivalry and adventure with which I followed behind the coach of my beloved, knowing I was heading to a place well known for intrigue, and lamenting only that I was not yet old enough to wear a gleaming sword at my belt with which to carve rivals into little pieces. I was a long way from imagining that, with time, my wishes would be fulfilled, point by point. But when the hour actually came for me to kill for Angélica de Alquézar—and I did kill for her—neither she nor I were children. All my romancing had ceased, and life was no longer a game.

Pardiez. I wander in circles, with digressions and leaps in time that take me away from the thread of my tale. So

I shall pick it up again by calling Your Mercies' attention to something central to my story: the enthusiasm at seeing my beloved that caused me to commit a careless act I would later deeply regret.

Ever since don Vicente de la Cruz's visit I had thought I detected the movement of suspicious people around our house. Nothing truly disturbing, it is true; only a couple of faces that were not usually seen either on Calle del Arcabuz or in the Tavern of the Turk. I suppose that this in itself was not overly strange, for on Cava Baja, as well as other streets in the neighborhood, there were a number of inns. But that morning I had noticed something I would have given more consideration to had I not been waiting for Angélica to pass by. It was only later that I gave it proper thought, when I had ample time to mull over the events that had brought me to the sinister place I found myself in. Or where, to be more accurate, I found myself forced to go.

It had happened that after we returned from the mass at the church of Las Benitas, I stood at the tavern door, and Diego Alatriste went on to Calle de los Correos, where he had business at the letter-office. And at that moment, as the captain was walking up Toledo, two strangers strolling past the fruit stands with an innocent air exchanged a few words in a low voice before one of them turned and followed the captain. I watched from where I was, wondering whether it was a chance move or whether the two were planning some thievery, when Angélica's carriage went by and erased everything but her from my mind. And yet, as I later had bitter opportunity to lament, the ear-to-ear mustaches, the wide-brimmed hats pulled down in swashbuckling fashion, the swords and daggers, and the swaggering walk of those two bullies, should have made me dog their steps. But God, the Devil, or whoever plays us life's pranks, always watches with amusement as through carelessness, pride, or ignorance, we find ourselves walking on the sharp edge of the knife.

She was as beautiful as Lucifer before his expulsion from Paradise. Her carriage had stopped beneath the poplar trees lining the road, and she had got out of the coach to stroll around the fountain. She had not yet outgrown her blond curls, and the lustrous cloth of her dress, as blue as her eyes, seemed to have been cut from the cloudless sky that framed the rooftops and towers of Madrid, its ancient wall, and the solid mass of the palace. After the coachman hobbled his mules, he had gone to join his fellow drivers, and the duenna had gone to fill a receptacle with water from the famed fountain. Angélica was alone. I felt my heart thumping as I drew closer beneath the trees, and from a distance I watched as she graciously greeted a few young friends who were having a little social, and then, after stealing a glance toward the distant chaperone, accepted a treat they offered her.

At that moment, I would have given all my youth and all my dreams to be, instead of a humble, beardless page, one of the dashing hidalgos—or at least men who resembled hidalgos—following the paths, twisting their mustaches as they sighted appealing señoritas, addressing a few clever words to them, hat in hand, fist elegantly posed on a hip or on the pommel of a sword. It was undoubtedly true that there were also ordinary folk there, no few of them, and with experience I learned that in those days, as in ours, not everything that glisters is good breeding, for there were whores and rogues among them who gave themselves airs out of vanity or a wish to improve their lot. Whatever their background, however dubious, Jew or Moor, it was enough to have bad handwriting, speak slowly and gravely, have debts, ride a horse, and carry a sword, in order to pass oneself off as a gentleman. But to my young eyes, anyone who wore a cape and sword—or clog shoes, fine petticoats, and farthingales—seemed to me to be a person of quality. At that point, I did not know much of the world.

A few dandies rode by on horseback, making their mounts rear and curvet as they neared a coach filled with ladies—or doxies—flirting with them whoever they were, and I wished with all my heart to be one of them, to rein in my horse and address Angélica in exquisite phrases. By now, she had penetrated deeper into the grove and, gathering up her underskirts with infinite grace, was meandering among the ferns that bordered the banks of the stream. Her eyes seemed to be fixed on the ground, and as I drew closer I could see that she was following the path of a long line of industrious ants scurrying back and forth with the discipline of German infantrymen. More venturesome than ever before, I took a few more steps in her direction before some twigs snapped beneath my feet. She looked up at me. Or it might be more accurate to say that the sky and her gown and her gaze enveloped me like a warm mist, and I felt my head whirl the way it did in the Tavern of the Turk from the vapors of wine spilled on the table, clouding my senses and making everything seem very slow and far away.

"I know you," she said.

She did not smile, nor did she seem surprised or displeased by my presence. She looked at me with curiosity, in the way that mothers and older sisters look before they say "You have grown a good inch," or "Your voice is changing." To my good fortune, I was wearing an old but clean doublet that had no patches, and passable breeches; also, following the captain's orders, I had washed my face and ears. I strove to pass her scrutiny without flinching, and after a brief struggle with my innate shyness, I was able to return her gaze serenely.

"My name is Íñigo Balboa," I said.

"I know. You are the friend of that Captain Triste, or Batristre."

She spoke with a very familiar tone, as she might to a friend or a servant. But she had said "friend" of the captain, and not "page" or "servant." More, she had remembered who I was. That alone—which in other circumstances might not be calming in the least, since my name or Alatriste's on the lips of the niece of Luis de Alquézar was more a promise of danger than cause for satisfaction—seemed to me completely adorable, making me happier than the gift of new doublet and breeches of Castile woolen. Angélica remembered my name. And with it, a portion of the life that I was resolved to place at her feet, sacrificing it to her without so much as blinking. I felt, and I wonder if you will truly know what I mean, like a man run through with a dagger: that I would live as long as it was not pulled out, and that removing it would kill me.

"Have you come for the healing waters?" I asked, to break the silence that the intensity of her gaze had made unbearable.

She wrinkled her nose and pouted. "I eat too many sweets," she said. Then she shrugged her shoulders in a childish way, as if that was a stupid concern. She looked toward the fountain where her duenna was standing talking with a acquaintance.

"It's ridiculous," she added scornfully.

I deduced that Angélica de Alquézar did not hold the highest regard for the dragon charged with looking after her, nor of the physics of physicians who with their bloodletting and remedies dispatched more Christians than the hangman of Seville.

"So I imagine," I replied courteously. "Everyone knows that sweets are good for one's health." I vaguely remembered having heard the pharmacist Fadrique say something similar in the tavern. "They build up the blood and the humors. I am sure that a honey bun, or a fritter, or custards, do more to stimulate melancholy humors than water from that fountain."

I stopped, hesitant to go any further, for I had exhausted my pharmaceutical knowledge.

"You have a funny accent," she said.

"It's Basque," I replied. "I was born in Oñate."

"I thought that Basques cut off their words," she said, and recited an old Basque saying, imitating their clipped speech: *"If you put down the lance and pick up the sword, soon you will see who has the last word . . ."*

She laughed. If it did not sound pretentious, I would

tell you that her laughter was argentine. It rang like the polished silver that artisans in the port of Guadalajara hang on the door of their shops on Corpus Christi feast day.

"'That is how persons from Biscay talk." I was unsure of the difference, but I was vaguely irritated. "Oñate is in Guipúzcoa."

I felt a compelling need to impress her, without the least notion of how. Clumsily, I tried to pick up the thread of my disquisition on the beneficial properties of sweets. I lowered my voice to sound more manly. "Now. In regard to melancholy humors . . ."

I was interrupted when a dog raced toward us, a large brown mastiff that had been charging about the area. Instinctively, I stepped between it and Angélica. The dog ran off without looking for a fight, as had the lion from don Quixote, and when I turned to look again, Angélica was observing me as she had when I first spoke, her curiosity apparent.

"And what do you know of my humors?"

A note of defiance resonated in her voice, and those intensely blue eyes had become very serious; there was no suggestion of a child in them. Those lips! Still parted after her question. That soft, rounded chin. Those blond spirals of curls touching shoulders covered with delicate Flemish lace. I was enslaved. I tried to swallow without being obvious.

"I know nothing, as yet," I replied, as candidly as I could. "But I know I would give my life for you."

I may have blushed as I spoke those words, but there are things you must say when it is time to say them, or risk regretting it all your life. Although what one may later regret is having spoken them at all.

"I would give my life," I repeated.

There was a long, thrilling silence. The chaperone was coming back, black beneath her white headgear, like a magpie of bad omen, with the flask of water in her hand. The dragon was about to retake possession of my damsel, so I started to leave, wanting to put distance between us. But Angélica was still studying me as if she were able to read my thoughts. She put her hands to her throat and pulled out a delicate gold chain with a small charm hanging from it. She undid the clasp, and put the chain in my hands.

"Perhaps one day you may die," she whispered.

As she spoke those words, her enigmatic eyes never left mine, and at the same time, a smile came to her lips. It was a smile so beautiful, so perfect, so filled with all the light in a Spanish sky vast as the abyss of her eyes, that I wanted to die that instant, sword in hand, shouting her name as there in Flanders my father had shouted the name of his king, his homeland, and his flag. After all was said and done, I thought, maybe those things were all one and the same.

IV. THE ASSAULT

Far in the distance, a dog barked four times, and after that . . . silence. Well armed, with pistol, sword, and dagger at his waist, Captain Alatriste looked at the moon that seemed about to impale itself upon the tower of Las Benitas convent, and then, turning his head from side to side, his eyes swept the shadowy corners of La Encarnación plaza. The coast was clear.

The captain adjusted his buffalo skin jerkin and tossed back the tails of the short cape over his shoulders. As if that had been a signal, three dark silhouettes emerged from the gloom, two from one side of the plaza and one from the other, and moved toward the convent wall. Light shone from one window; almost immediately it was extinguished, then quickly relighted.

"It is she," whispered don Francisco de Quevedo.

He was stationed beside the wall, all in black—hat, clothing, and cape—and he had not drunk a drop all night despite the chill—in order, he said, to have a steady hand. I could not see him, but I heard him slowly draw his sword halfway from its scabbard and then let it drop back, testing whether it moved smoothly. And I also heard him mutter a few words of his own composition:

"Night could not overcome my sorrows
nor give peace to my vexations . . ."

I wondered briefly whether don Francisco was reciting verse to relieve his anxiety, to counter the cold, or whether he truly had ice in his veins and was capable of composing poems at the very Gates of Hell. Whatever the case, this was not the time to give the proper due to the flower of his satiric genius. My attention was focused on the captain, whose dark profile, masked by shadow, was still as a statue beneath the broad brim of his hat. The three dark shapes that had slipped across the plaza earlier were also frozen, attempting to remain unseen. The dog barked again, only twice this time, and from the hill of Los Caños del Peral came, as answer, the faint nickers of the mules of the waiting coach. With that sound, Diego Alatriste turned toward me. His eyes were palest gray in the moonlight.

"Be very cautious," he said.

He put his hand on my shoulder. I took a deep breath and bolted across the plaza, feeling like the boy who stuck his head in the wolf's mouth, aware of the captain's eyes on me. In my ears, the homage don Francisco was kind enough to improvise, rewriting some verses of his own:

*"How easily he scales the high wall of stone
spurred on by his youth."*

My heart was pounding as hard as it had earlier that day when I had been so close to Angélica de Alquézar. Or perhaps more. I felt an almost unbearable tightness in my stomach and my throat, and unfamiliar drums were sounding in my ears as I passed the crouching shapes of don Vicente de la Cruz and his two sons. They were huddled against the wall, and I could see the glint of metal from between the folds of their capes.

"Quickly, lad," whispered the father, impatient.

I nodded, and followed the wall toward the carriage guard at the corner. There I surreptitiously crossed myself, commending myself to the same God whose holy sanctuary I was about to violate. With no difficulty at all—at the time I was as agile as a monkey—I climbed up onto the pillar, then, teetering slightly on its narrow ledge, I reached for the wall and pulled myself up. I sat there an instant, astride, bent low so as not to be silhouetted against the moonlight. On one side below were the street and the plaza, and the silent shapes of my companions hugging the wall; on the other lay the shadowy silence of Las Benitas's garden, broken only by the intermittent chirping of a cricket. I waited until the beating of my heart faded from my eardrums before moving again. And when I did, I felt the charm Angélica de Alquézar had given me at the Acero fountain swing out from inside my shirt, and heard the *chink!* as it struck stone.

I had spent hours studying it. It looked very old, and on it were engraved some strange and fascinating symbols.

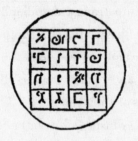

I stuffed the amulet back into my shirt, where it lay against my bare skin, hoping and praying that it would bring me the luck I would need in this venture. The branches of the nearest apple tree scratched my face as I swung forward onto a limb and then, after hanging by my hands a few seconds, dropped the six or seven feet to the ground. I fell and rolled, without significant damage,

brushed the dirt from my clothing, and, praying to the Holy
Mother of God that there were no unchained dogs about,
I followed the wall back to the small door and carefully
drew back the bolt. The moment it was open, don Vicente
de la Cruz and his sons slipped inside, wrapped in capes and
weapons drawn, and ran quickly across the garden, their
steps muffled by the soft earth. As for me, my job was done.

I had played my part like a lad with real backbone.
Without adventures, we would never know our heroes. So
I went back out to the street, well satisfied, and unhesitat-
ingly crossed the plaza. The captain's instructions had been
very precise: Go right home by the shortest route. Leaving
Las Benitas and La Encarnación behind, I started up the
hill along the low parapet, serene and swollen with pride
because everything had been as smooth as silk. Then I was
struck by the temptation to linger just a bit near the waiting coach in order to glimpse the rescued damsel—if only
by moonlight and for an instant—when her father and
brothers spirited her away.

I hesitated a moment, torn between discipline and indulgence: a struggle that was never concluded. For it was
in that moment of irresolution that I heard the first shot.

There were at least ten of them, Diego Alatriste calculated, as he unsheathed his dagger and his sword. And in

the patio of the convent, a few more. They came from every direction. From dark corners and doorways, from the street and the plaza, burnished steel gleamed and cries of "Hold! By the authority of the Inquisition!" and "In the name of the King!" thundered through the night. More shots sounded inside the convent wall, and a tangle of figures and flashing swords could be seen at the small door. For a moment, Alatriste thought he glimpsed a novice's white headdress amid the clashing blades, but that image was erased by the flash of more pistol shots.

Furthermore, it was the moment to look after his own health. The cry "By the authority of the Inquisition!" was enough to make anyone's blood run cold. But now he was fighting to save his skin, and in such circumstances it mattered little whether against the Inquisition or the magistrate's constables: throat slashed by a secular dagger, or sprinkled with holy water; neither was desirable. With his dagger he blocked a thrust from a shadow that seemed to have materialized out of nowhere. He drove back the apparition with three two-handed slashes and an oath, and out of the corner of his eye saw don Francisco de Quevedo fending off another two men. It scarcely seemed necessary—and it would have cost him precious breath needed for other purposes—to yell "We've been betrayed," or something of the kind, so don Francisco and the captain applied themselves to their task, keeping their mouths more or less closed. Whoever the responsible party might be, it was clearly an ambush, and there was nothing to do now but make them pay with their lights.

The man Alatriste had driven off closed in again, and the captain, perceiving the flash of the enemy blade, set his feet, and just in time parried a patinando. He took one step forward, then another, clasped the adversary's sword between his elbow and ribs, thrust his own forward, and heard the rewarding cry when his blade sliced across his opponent's face. Fortunately, the champions of the Inquisition were not as skilled as Amadis of Gaul, and that was what turned the tide.

Alatriste stepped back in the darkness until his back was to a wall, and seized the brief respite to see how don Francisco was faring. The poet, faithful to his proven skill, limping and cursing under his breath, was holding his two attackers at bay. But reinforcements were arriving, and soon the friends would not have hands enough to butcher so much meat. Fortunately, most of the attackers were clustered near the convent wall, where the confusion and yelling were increasing by the minute. It was obvious that don Vicente de la Cruz and his sons were candidates for memorials. The captain smelled the acrid odor of lighted fuses.

"We have no choice but to flee," he bellowed to don Francisco, trying to make himself heard above the *cling, cling, clang* of blades.

"Precisely what I have been attempting to do," the poet shouted in return, between mighty slashes. "For some time now!"

He had dispatched one of his adversaries and was retreating parallel to the wall, with the second swordsman tight to his blade. A new shadow suddenly appeared before Alatriste, or perhaps it was the man he had driven off, returning now with the legions of Mohammed to wreak vengeance for the affront to his face. Sparks flew as sword clashed against sword and against stone. The captain, left arm held to protect his face, waited until his adversary shifted his feet for a better line of engagement, then lunged forward and landed a staggering kick. He lashed out with sword, dagger, and again sword. When his enemy tried to stand upright, at least half the captain's blade was protruding from his back.

"Blessed Mary, Mother of God," he heard the man mutter, air escaping as Alatriste pulled the sword from his chest. He blasphemed, again invoked the Virgin, and dropped to his knees beside the wall, as his sword fell between his thighs with a metallic ring.

In front of the convent, a dark figure broke swiftly from the swirl of figures. Then came the fire from the harquebuses, and street and plaza were alight in a fiesta of rockets and gunpowder. Balls whizzed past the captain and don Francisco, and one flattened itself on the wall between them.

"Fuck," said Quevedo.

This was not a time for meter and rhyme. And men were still arriving. Alatriste, wet with sweat beneath the buffcoat that had already saved him from at least three wounds that night, looked around, searching for the best way to escape. As don Francisco retreated from his assailant, he backed into the captain. The poet had had the identical thought. Escape.

"Let every dog," said Quevedo, panting, between a feint and a thrust, "lick his own bollocks."

His second adversary was by now rolling, wounded, at his feet, but a third had come along, and don Francisco was getting winded. The captain, who was less engaged, clamped his dagger between his teeth, and with his left hand pulled his pistol from his belt; when he was but a handspan from the enemy harassing the poet, he fired a shot that blew away half the man's jaw. The flash of the shot temporarily stopped any who were thinking of joining the fray, so, taking advantage of the interruption, and not awaiting an invitation, don Francisco, very spry despite his lameness, broke away, running fleetly.

After waiting a few seconds to further discourage anyone who might follow, Alatriste did the same, choosing for his retreat an alleyway that he had scouted out earlier. This was the custom of veteran soldiers, who establish escape routes before a combat, for when a bad card is dealt, there is not always sufficient time or clarity of judgment to make such useful appraisals. The narrow street he had chosen ran beneath an arch and ended at a wall that he easily leapt over, landing on a chicken coop and waking the hens. Someone lighted a lantern and shouted something from a window; by then the captain was across the courtyard, tripping in the darkness but without hurting himself. After climbing over a fence, he was free and in a reasonably good state of health, except for a few scratches and a mouth drier than the sand dunes at Nieuwpoort. He found a dark corner where he could catch his breath, wondering whether don Franciso de Quevedo had gotten away safely. Once he could hear something besides his own gasping, he listened carefully: no shots or yells from the direction of the convent.

No one, *pardiez*, would give a *maravedí* for the skin of don Vicente de la Cruz and his sons. In the little likely case that one of them was left alive.

He heard running, like that of armed men, and there was a glare of lanterns at the corner. Then all was silent again. Rested, and in command of himself, he lingered a long while in the darkness. He was trembling; the sweat beneath his buffcoat was now chill, but he paid little attention. He kept turning over and over the question of who had set that trap for them.

The shots and the clanging blades had made me retrace my steps, as I asked myself what could be happening in La Encarnación plaza. I started running back toward it, but prudence quickly gained the upper hand. *He who loses his head*—goes one of the soldiers' sayings I had learned from the captain—*ends up really losing that head,* often with the unwelcome assistance of a rope. So I stopped, with my heart jumping out of my breast, as I tried to decide what was the best thing to do. Would I be a help or a hindrance to my friends?

That was the situation when I heard the sound of running footsteps and the hair-raising cry of "By the authority of the Inquisition!" which in that day, as I have already recounted to Your Mercies, would raise gooseflesh on the most villainous of men. It spurred me to action, I can assure you, and with the greatest caution, I had in a trice taken refuge behind the low stone parapet that served as a kind of railing down the length of the hill. I had scarcely got my breath back from my scramble over the wall when I heard footsteps nearby, more shots and cries, and the clash of steel. I had put aside my concerns about the fate of the captain and don Francisco and begun to worry about my own, when a body came tumbling over the low wall beside me.

I was ready to sprint from that place like a hare, but the new arrival uttered a mournful moan that made me turn and look at him. There was enough moonlight that I was able to recognize the younger of the two de la Cruz brothers, the one called don Luis, who had fled from the convent badly wounded. As I went toward him, he staggered to his feet and looked at me with frightened eyes that glowed feverishly in the scant light. I ran my fingers over his face, as blind men do to recognize people, and he fell toward me, prey to something that for an instant I took to be a faint, but, when I put out my hands to steady him, I learned was loss of blood from his wounds. Don Luis was perforated with stabs and shot from a harquebus, and when he collapsed into my arms I smelled sweat mixed with the sickeningly sweet scent of blood.

"Help me, boy," he murmured.

He had spoken so quietly that I could barely hear his words, and the breath it cost him to speak seemed to have weakened him further. I tried to get him to stand, pulling him by one arm, but he was very heavy and his wounds made him nearly lifeless. All I got from him was a prolonged moan of pain. He had lost his sword, and the only weapon he had left was the dagger at his waist—I had touched the grip when I tried to lift him.

"Help me," he repeated.

In his present state, he seemed much younger, closer to my own age; and everything that had impressed me earlier, his elegance and charm, had vanished completely. He was older than I, and a handsome man, but he had as many holes as a sieve. I was unhurt, and his only hope, which made me feel strangely responsible. So, restraining my natural inclination to leave him there and look for safe haven as fast as my legs could carry me, I stayed on.

I pressed as close to him as I could, pulled his arms around my neck, and tried to lift him onto my back, but he was limp and slippery from his own blood. I swiped my hand over my face, despairing, and as I did, bathed myself with the viscous liquid dripping on me. Don Luis had fallen back again against the stone wall, and was now suffering very little. I tried to feel for one of the large holes through which his soul was escaping, thinking I would plug it with a linen handkerchief I had pulled from my pouch, but by the time I found a hole and put my fingers in it—like Doubting Saint Thomas—I knew that it was futile, and that the young man was not going to see the dawn.

I felt unnaturally lucid. *It is time to get going, Íñigo,* I told myself. The shots and the din had faded from the plaza, and the silence, if possible, was even more menacing. Again I thought of the captain and don Francisco. By now they could be dead, imprisoned, or fleeing; none of the three possibilities was encouraging, however much my confidence in the poet's sword and my master's serenity inclined me to believe they were safely away or taking refuge in one of the few churches open at this early morning hour.

I got up slowly. Luis de la Cruz was on the ground, curled into a ball and no longer moaning. He was dying, and all I heard was his breathing, growing steadily weaker and more irregular, punctuated from time to time by a sinister gargle. He was not strong enough to ask me to help him or to call me "boy." He was drowning in his own blood, which was spreading slowly into a large dark pool gleaming in the light of the moon.

A single shot from a pistol or harquebus rang out in the distance, as if it had been fired at someone being pursued, and I clung to that sound, hoping it might have been aimed—unsuccessfully—at the fleet shadow of Captain Alatriste running to safety in the darkness. As for my own young hide, it was time to find sanctuary for it. So once more I bent over the dying man. I pulled out the dagger that would be of no help to him in his journey, and stood up, ready to quit that unhappy place.

But, could that be music? A kind of *ti-ri-tu, ta-ta* from someone whistling behind me. The sound turned me to ice, and my fingers, sticky with the blood of Luis de la Cruz, tightened on his dagger grip. I turned very slowly, holding the dagger high, and as I did, moonlight glanced from the blade. At the far end of the low stone wall was a familiar shape: a dark silhouette cloaked in a cape and a black wide-brimmed hat. Recognizing who it was, I knew that the trap was lethal, and that I had sprung it.

"So, boy, we meet again," said the shadow.

Gualterio Malatesta's gruff, grating voice resounding in the silence of the night was a sentence of death. Your Mercies will ask why the Devil I stood there, flat-footed, instead of flying out of there like a soul in the arms of the Devil—or one fleeing from him. The reasons are two. For one, the Italian's appearance had left me as frozen as a post sunk in the ground; the second, my enemy was standing directly in the path I had to take to escape the pocket where poor Luis de la Cruz lay. Whatever the reason, there I was, holding the dagger before me as Malatesta calmly looked me over, as if he were already at the Gates of Hell.

"We meet again," he repeated.

Then he moved away from the wall, almost as if too lazy to stir himself, and took a step toward me. Only one. I could see that his sword was still in the scabbard. I shifted my dagger slightly, and again it gleamed softly between us.

"Give that to me," he said.

I clenched my teeth but did not answer. I did not want him to know how frightened I was. Beside me, on the ground, the dying man uttered one last moan, and then, no more death rattles. Ignoring my naked blade, Malatesta took two more steps in my direction, and bent down with interest.

"Less work for the hangman."

As he spoke, he prodded the dead youth with one foot. Then he turned back toward me. Despite the darkness, I could tell he was surprised to see me still holding the dagger.

"Drop it, boy," he muttered, almost as if I weren't there.

Now I could see other shadows, armed men coming toward us; and yes, *they* were carrying pistols and unsheathed daggers and swords. Light shone around the corner, beamed above our heads, and started down the hill. I watched the black shadow of the Italian gliding across Luis de la Cruz. The young man lay motionless, curled up on the ground. Had it not been for the open eyes staring straight ahead, I would have said he had fallen asleep in a large red puddle.

The lantern was coming closer, and now Malatesta's

shadow fell on me. He was silhouetted against the light, and metallic reflections sparked off the approaching men. Still I had not lowered the dagger. And when the lantern stopped beside us, it lighted one side of the Italian's thin, pockmarked and scarred face, reminding me of a sinister moonscape. Above his mustache, which he wore trimmed in a thin line, eyes as black as his clothing studied me with amused attention.

"You are a prisoner of the Holy Inquisition, boy," he said, and in his mouth the terrible words, accompanied by a smile that was pure menace, sounded like a mockery.

I was too terrified to reply or to move, so I did neither. I stood stock-still, the dagger held high. I imagine that to anyone looking on, my inaction could have been interpreted as resolve. That may have been why I caught a flash of curiosity, or interest, in my enemy's black gaze. Almost immediately, some of the constables encircling us made a move to take me, but Malatesta stopped them with a gesture. Then, slowly, as if giving me the opportunity to reflect, he drew his sword from the sheath: an enormous sword with an interminable blade, huge quillons, and a wide guard. He contemplated that blade for a few instants, then slowly raised it until it glittered before me. Compared with that monster, my dagger seemed ridiculous.

But it was my dagger. And so, although my arm was beginning to feel as if it were made of lead, I held it steady, not flinching, staring into the eyes of the Italian like someone hypnotized by a snake.

"The lad has gall."

I heard laughter from among the shadows behind the lantern. Malatesta reached out with his sword and ticked the tip of my dagger. The sound made the hair rise on the back of my neck.

"Now drop it," he said.

Again someone laughed, and that laughter fired my blood. I swung with all my might, hoping to rip Malatesta's sword from his hand, and the sound rang out like a challenge. Suddenly, before I could react, I saw the tip of his sword two inches from my face, motionless, as if he were considering whether or not to run me through. Again I struck out with the dagger, but his blade had disappeared and I swung into empty space.

There was renewed laughter. I felt an infinite sorrow, a grief that brought tears, not to my eyes—which my pride kept dry—but to my heart and throat. And I learned that there are some things no man can tolerate though it cost him his life or, precisely, because that life would not be worth living if he yielded. And in my sadness I remembered the hills and green fields of my childhood, and chimney smoke on the damp morning air, and the memory of my father's hard, rough hands, the scratchy whisper of his soldier's mustache the day he embraced me for the last time—I being but a boy—as he went off to meet his fate below the walls of Julich. And I felt the warmth of our hearth, and I could see the figure of my mother bent over by the fire, sewing, or cooking, and hear the laughter of my little sisters playing nearby. And I longed desperately for the warmth of my bed on a cold winter morning. And then it was the sky, blue as Angélica de Alquézar's eyes, that I longed to have overhead when life ended—rather than darkness and lantern light, so somber and sad. But no one chooses his moment, and this was, without doubt, mine.

I am going to die, I told myself. And with all the vigor of my thirteen years, and all the desperation of the many beautiful things that I would now never know, ever, I focused on the gleaming tip of the enemy steel and commended my soul to God, clumsily, with a quick prayer my mother had taught me in her Basque tongue as soon as I could speak. Then, sure that my father would welcome me with widespread arms and a smile of pride on his lips, I gripped the dagger, closed my eyes, and, blindly swinging, threw myself against Gualterio Malatesta's sword.

I lived. Later, every time I tried to remember that moment, I could re-create it only through a rapid succession of sensations: the last glint of the sword before me, the fatigue in my arm raining blows right and left, my forward lunge toward nothing, not sword, not pain, not resistance. Then suddenly, contact with a solid, hard body, and clothing, a strong hand restraining me, or rather embracing me as if fearing I would hurt myself. And trying to free my arm to use the dagger, and as I struggled without a sound, a voice with a vaguely Italian accent whispering, "Easy there, easy!" almost with tenderness, pinning me as if I were going to wound myself with my own weapon. And then, as I kept swinging, with my face buried in dark cloth that smelled a little of sweat and a little of leather and metal, the hand that seemed to embrace or protect me slowly twisted my arm, not cruelly, until I had to drop the dagger. Near tears, and wishing I could cry, I seized that arm with rage, like a pit bull ready to die on the spot. And I did not let go until that same hand closed into a fist, and a blow behind my ear shattered the night into a thousand pieces, and I sank into a sudden deep and brutal sleep. A black, bottomless void that I fell into without a cry or a moan, prepared to meet my Maker, like a good soldier.

Later I dreamed that I hadn't died.

And I was terrified by the certainty that I was going to wake up.

V. IN GOD'S NAME

I awakened suddenly, hurting all over, in the darkness of a moving coach with drawn curtains. I felt a strange weight around my wrists, and when I moved, heard a metallic clicking that filled me with dread. My wrists were secured with iron cuffs, and they in turn were fastened by a chain to the floor of the coach. Through chinks in the curtains I glimpsed light, and learned that it was well past dawn. Whatever the actual time, I had no idea how long it had been since I was captured. The carriage was moving at a normal pace, and at times, on a hill, I would hear the crack of a whip and shouts of the coachman as he laid into the mules. I also heard the sound of horses' hooves, dropping back and then catching up. I was being driven, then, out of the city, chained, and with an escort. And according to what I had heard when taken prisoner, I had fallen into the clutches of the Inquisition. I did not have to stretch my imagination to conclude the obvious: If anyone had a black future ahead of him, it was I.

I wept. I burst into disconsolate tears in the dark pitching of the carriage. No one could see me there. I cried until I had no tears left, and then, snuffling, I pushed back into a corner to wait, rigid with fright. Like every Spaniard of the time, I had heard enough about the practices of the Inquisition—that sinister shadow that had loomed over our lives for years and years and years—to know my destination: the dreaded secret dungeons of the Holy Office, in Toledo.

I am sure, Your Mercies, that I have spoken of the Inquisition. One thing I know: it was no worse here than in other countries of Europe, although the Dutch, English, French, and Lutherans, who were our natural enemies, proclaimed it part of the infamous Black Legend they called upon to justify the sacking of the Spanish empire in the hour of her decline. True it is that the Holy Office, which was created to guard the orthodoxy of the Faith, was more rigorous in Spain than in Italy and Portugal, for example, and worse yet in the Antilles. But the Inquisition also existed other places. And furthermore, with that excuse or without it, the Germans, French, and English sent more non-believers, witches, and wretched poor up in smoke than all the victims burned at the stake in Spain.

Here, thanks to the punctilious bureaucracy of the Austrian monarchy, each and every human they turned to cracklings—many, but not all that many—was duly recorded under history of trial, name, and surname. Something that cannot be claimed by the vile frogs of the most Christian King of France, the accursed heretics farther north, or an eternally treacherous, vile, and piratical England. For when *they* got their fires going, they did it joyfully and wholeheartedly, with no order or harmony, and according to whim and self-interest—damned, hypocritical swine. Added to that, secular justice was as cruel as its ecclesiastical counterpart, and the general public equally so, owing to a lack of culture and the masses' fondness for seeing neighbors drawn and quartered.

It is also the fact that the Inquisition often acted as an arm of the government under such kings as our fourth Philip, who left in its hands the oversight of new Christians and Jewish sympathizers, the persecution of witches, bigamists, and sodomites, even the authority to censor books and combat the smuggling of weapons, horses, and legal and counterfeit currency. The latter responsibility was due to the argument that smugglers and counterfeiters greatly harmed the interests of the monarchy, and he who was enemy of the monarchy—the defender of the Faith—was also, to keep it short and simple, the enemy of God.

Nevertheless, despite the slander of foreigners, and even though not all trials were resolved at the stake and one might find examples of piety and justice, the Inquisition, like any excessive power placed in the hands of man, was ominous. And the decadence we Spanish were suffering across the world—seeds that produced, and will continue to produce, fields of thistles and nettles—can be explained, primarily, by suppression of liberty, cultural isolation, loss of confidence, and the religious obscurantism created by the Holy Office. So great was the fear it spread that even collaborating agents of the Inquisition, its so-called "family"—a post that could be bought—enjoyed complete immunity. To say the words "a *familiar* of the Holy Office" was the same as saying spy or informer, and of those there were some twenty thousand in the Spain of our Catholic Philip.

Your Mercies should be aware of what the Inquisition meant in a country like ours, in which a charging bull could not move Justice as quickly as pieces of eight, where everything up to the Most Holy Sacrament was for sale, and where, in addition, every man and woman alive had a quarrel to be adjudged. No two Spaniards—and by my faith this is still the case—took their breakfast chocolate the same way: one drank only chocolate from Oaxaca; another took his black; this one with milk; that one with fried bread; and yet another in a bowl with sweet French bread. Similarly, it was necessary no longer to *be* a good Catholic and old Christian, but only to *appear* to be. And nothing made one seem a more enthusiastic defender of the Faith than to betray those who were not, or those who because of old rancor, jealousy, envy, or quarrels made good prospects. Who knows? Some of those prospects might actually be nonbelievers.

As was to be expected, denunciations fell like rain, and "I have it on good authority" and "Everyone knows" rattled down like hail. When the implacable finger of the Holy Office pointed toward some poor wretch, he immediately found himself abandoned by patrons, friends, and relatives. Son accused father, wife accused husband, and prisoner betrayed accomplices, or invented them, if he hoped to escape torture and death.

And there was I, at thirteen, trapped in that sinister web, knowing what awaited me and not daring to think about it. I knew stories of people who had taken their own lives to escape the horror of the prison I was being carried to. I must confess that in that dark carriage, I came to understand why. It would have been easier and more dignified, my thoughts ran, had I speared myself on Gualterio Malatesta's sword and ended everything quickly and cleanly.

But there was little doubt that Divine Providence wished me to suffer this test. Curled in my corner, I sighed deeply, resigned to confronting what lay ahead without hope of rescue.

Although it would not have hurt my feelings, I mused, had Providence, divine or otherwise, assigned that Herculean labor to someone else.

During the rest of the journey I thought of Captain Alatriste. I hoped with all my soul that he was safe, maybe somewhere nearby, planning to free me. But I did not hold that hope long. Even if he had escaped the extremely clever trap set by his enemies, this was not a chivalric romance filled with fabulous feats of knight-errantry; the shackles clicking to the swaying of the coach were not fantasy but real. And so, too, were my fear and loneliness, and my uncertain fate. Or certain, according to the point of view. The fact is that later, life—the passing years, adventures, loves, and the wars of our lord and king—caused me to lose faith in many things. But I had already, young as I was at the time, ceased to believe in miracles.

The carriage came to a stop. I heard the coachman unhitch the mules, and knew that we had stopped at a post house. I was trying to calculate where we might be when the coach door opened. The sudden glare dazzled me—for it was now the late afternoon of the next day—and for a few seconds I was blinded. I rubbed my eyes, and when I opened them, there stood Gualterio Malatesta, observing me. As always, he was in severe black: gloves and boots, the plume in his hat, and the line of mustache that accentuated the fineness of his features, forcing the contrast between the first impression of pulchritude and, at closer look, a face so marred by pockmarks and scars that it suggested a battlefield. At his back, across a broad sweep of land and about half a league away, I could see Toledo glowing in the golden light of the setting sun, its ancient walls crowned by the palace of Emperor Charles V.

"We say good-bye here, boy," said Malatesta.

I stared at him, confused. I must have looked terrible, with the dried blood of poor Luis de la Cruz all over my face and clothing, along with the usual wear of a journey. For a moment, I thought I saw a frown on the Italian's brow, as if he was not happy with my state, or my situation. I simply stared, uncomprehending.

"They take over here," he added finally.

He nearly smiled that slow, cruel, and dangerous smile of his that revealed teeth as white as the eyeteeth of a wolf. But it vanished immediately, as if he had changed his mind. Perhaps he judged that I was already so browbeaten that he would not humiliate me further. Actually, he did not seem all that comfortable. He observed me a moment longer, and then, his expression unreadable, put his hand on the door.

"Where are they taking me?" I asked.

My voice sounded weak, so unfamiliar it could have belonged to someone else. The Italian did not answer. His eyes, black as death, stared at me without blinking. When Gualterio Malatesta looked at you, you always wondered if he had eyelids.

"There."

With his chin, he gestured toward the city over his shoulder. I saw his hand on the door as the hand of the executioner, and the door as the stone on my tomb. I tried to find some way to prolong what instinct told me was to be my last moment of sunlight for a while.

"Why? What have I done?"

Again he did not answer. He simply stared. I could hear mules being brought up, and as they harnessed the new pair the carriage shook. I saw several men, armed to the teeth, pass behind the Italian, and in their midst the black and white robes of a pair of Dominican priests. One glanced toward me as he went by, indifferent, as if instead of seeing a human he were observing an object. That look was the most frightening thing I had as yet experienced.

"I am sorry, boy," said Malatesta.

He seemed to have read the horror in my thoughts. And may the Devil take me if in that moment I did not believe he was sincere. It was but an instant, however—those four words and a flash in the blackness of his gaze. When I tried to pursue the shred of compassion I thought I had glimpsed, I met only the impassive mask of an assassin. The carriage door was beginning to close.

"What news of the captain?" I asked with anguish, frantic to stay a few more instants in the sun.

Not another word from Gualterio Malatesta. A beam of sunlight shone on his somber face. And then I did see an expression I could not doubt, a quick flash of rage and spite. It lasted only a second, and then it was gone, hidden behind the cruel grimace, the dangerous, bloodthirsty smile that twisted his pale, cold lips. But my heart leaped with joy, for I knew, with every bone in my body, that Diego Alatriste had eluded the ambush.

Malatesta slammed the carriage door, and I was again in darkness. I heard shouted orders, a horse galloping away, and then the coachman's whip. The mules started off, and the carriage began to roll toward a place where not even God would be on my side.

The hopelessness of being in the hands of an all-powerful apparatus devoid of emotion, and thereby of pity, struck me the moment I emerged from the coach into a dismal inner courtyard that dusk made even more somber. After my shackles were removed, I was led to an underground room by four constables of the Holy Office and the two Dominicans I had seen at the post house.

I will spare Your Mercies the details, but after I was stripped and thoroughly searched, I was subjected to a preliminary interrogation by a scribe who demanded to know my name, age, the names of my father and mother, those of my four grandparents and eight great-grandparents, my current dwelling, and my place of origin. Then, in a routine tone, the scribe tested me on elementary Christian knowledge by making me recite the Lord's Prayer and the Ave Maria. Finally, he asked me the names of any persons who might be connected with my situation.

I asked what my situation *was*, but he did not tell me. I asked why I was there, and he did not answer that either. When he persisted in asking for names, I did not answer, pretending to be confused and afraid—although if I am to be frank, I didn't need to pretend. When my questioner persisted, I burst into tears, and that seemed to be enough for the moment, for he put his quill into the inkwell, scattered powder over the page, and put away his sheets of paper. On the strength of that experience, I resolved to resort to weeping any time I found myself in a tight spot, although I feared that weeping would not require any great effort on my part. If there was one thing I would not lack for, I surmised in my misery, it would be reason for shedding tears.

After that, believing the interview was over, I found it had been only a proem, a prologue: the first act had not yet begun. This I learned when I was taken into a square room without windows or embrasures, lit by a large candelabrum. The only furnishings were a large table, another smaller one holding writing materials, and a few benches. The two priests I'd seen at the post house were seated at the large table, along with a third individual wearing a large gold cross around his neck. With his dark beard and black robe he looked convincingly like an officer of the court, or a judge. At the smaller table was a scribe very different from the one who had conducted the preliminary questioning, a crowlike man who put down the smallest detail of what was said, and, to my growing fear, probably things I had not said. Two constables, one tall and strong-looking and the other redheaded and thin, were my guards. On the wall hung an enormous crucifix, the occupant of which had undoubtedly passed through the hands of this very tribunal.

As I learned from that point on, the most fearsome thing about being a prisoner in the secret dungeons of the Inquisition was that no one told you what your crime had been, or what proof or witnesses they had against you—

nothing about anything. The inquisitors limited themselves to posing question after question, and the scribe to
noting it all down, while you addled your brain trying to
decide whether what you were saying weighed on the side
of your release or of your condemnation. It was possible to
spend weeks, months, even years there without knowing
the exact reasons, with the added aggravation that if your
answers were not satisfactory, they would resort to torture
in order to facilitate your confession and obtain the proofs
they needed. And when you were tortured, you would begin to answer willy-nilly, not knowing what you should be
saying. Everything led to desperation, to the conscious or
unconscious betrayal of friends, of you yourself, and at
times to madness and death. That was one way of dying
other than being led in your white robe and conical hat to
the scaffold, with a garotte around your neck, a pyre of dry
kindling beneath your feet, and your neighbors and former friends shouting their approval, enchanted with the
spectacle.

I did at least know why I was there, though there was
little consolation in the knowledge. And because I knew
that, after the first questions, I soon found myself in serious straits. Especially when the younger priest, the one
who had glanced at me with such indifference, asked for
the names of my accomplices.

"Accomplices in what, *Ilustrísimo*?"

"I am not called *Ilustrísimo*," he replied darkly, his large tonsured bald spot gleaming in the light from the candelabrum. "I am asking for the names of your accomplices in the sacrilege."

The roles had been assigned, as in a play. While the man with the dark beard and black cloak sat in silence, like a judge who listens and deliberates before handing out his sentence, the two priests were skillfully playing their parts: the younger, the role of implacable inquisitor; the other, plumper and more placid in expression, the benevolent confidant. But I had lived in Madrid long enough to smell a ruse, so I determined not to trust either one, and to act as if I didn't see the man in the black robe.

An added complication was that I did not know how much they knew. And I hadn't the least idea whether my sacrilege—as it had just been defined—was the one they were referring to. Because, in talking with someone who has the power to make you regret it, it is just as dangerous to ask for one card too few as one card too many. Indeed, it can be ruinous even to say, "I'll stay."

"I have no accomplices, Reverend Father." I addressed the plump one, but with little hope. "Nor have I committed a sacrilege."

"You deny," the younger asked, "that in the company of others you profaned the convent of the Adoratrices Benitas?"

Well, that was something, even if that something gave me gooseflesh when I imagined the consequences. It was a specific accusation. I denied it, of course. And following that, I denied knowing—even by sight—the wounded man whom, on my way home, I had accidentally run into behind the low wall on Caños del Peral hill. I also denied that I had resisted arrest by the agents of the Holy Office. I denied everything to the end, everything I could, except the unarguable fact that I had been holding a dagger when the long arm of the Inquisition reached out to pull me in, and that another man's blood still crusted my doublet. As it was impossible to deny that, I plunged into a maze of circumlocutions and explanations that had no bearing on the case. Finally I unleashed the tears, as a last resort in fending off new questions.

That tribunal, however, had seen many tears fall, so the priests, the man in the robe, and the scribe simply waited until my jeremiad had ended. It appeared that they had time to burn—not a direction I wanted my thoughts to take—and that, aside from their indifference, neither cruel nor reproachful, and their asking the same questions over and over with monotonous persistence, was the most disquieting aspect of the interrogation. Although I tried to maintain the air of nonchalance and confidence appropriate for an innocent, that was what terrified me about those men: their coldness and their patience. After a dozen "No" and "I don't know," even the plump cleric had dropped his mask, and it was obvious that I would have to travel many leagues to find a hint of compassion.

I had not eaten a bite in more than twenty-four hours, and I was beginning to feel faint, even though I was seated on a bench. Having exhausted the ploy of the tears, I began to consider the possibilities of a faint. Considering the way I was feeling, it would not be a pretense. That was when the priest said something that hurtled me toward an honest swoon.

"What do you know of one Diego Alatriste y Tenorio, often known as Captain Alatriste?"

This is it, Íñigo, I thought. The end. End of denials, and pointless blather. From here on, anything you say, even what you confirm or disprove before that scribe who is setting down your every last sigh, can be used against the captain. So you are through talking, let that take you where it takes you. Despite my situation and my whirling head, and despite the boundless panic sinking its claws into my entrails, I decided, calling upon my last shreds of strength, that nothing, not those priests, not the secret dungeons, not the Supreme Council, not the Pope of Rome, would tear a word from me that would endanger Captain Alatriste.

"Answer the question," the younger priest ordered.

I did not. I concentrated on the floor before me, on a

paving stone split by a crack with as many sharp turns as my luck. And I was staring at the same crack when one of the constables standing behind me, obeying an order issued by the priest without a change of expression, stepped forward and struck a blow to the nape of my neck that was like being clubbed. From the force of it, I calculated that it came from the taller and stronger of the two.

"Answer the question," the priest repeated.

I stared at the crack without a peep, and was stunned by a blow stronger than the first. Tears as sincere as the pain in my bruised neck flowed despite my attempt to contain them. I swiped them away with the back of my hand; this was not the moment I wanted to cry.

"Answer the question."

I bit my lips so there would be no chance I would open my mouth, and saw the crack in the floor speeding toward me as my eardrums rang, *boom*, like the tympanum of a drum. This time the constable had knocked me to the ground. And the stones were as cold as the voice I heard above me.

"Answer the question."

The words came from a great distance, like echoes in a bad dream. A hand pulled me onto my back, and I saw the face of the redheaded guard bending over me, and behind him, that of the priest who had been questioning me. I could not contain a moan of desperation and hopelessness, because I knew that nothing would get me out of that place, and that they had all the time in the world. As for me, I had barely started down the road I was going to travel to hell, and I was in no rush to continue. So I fainted, just as the redhead had grabbed my doublet to drag me to my feet. And—I call as witness the Christ looking down on me from the wall—this time I did not have to feign at all.

I do not know how many hours went by in the damp cell where my only company was an enormous rat that spent its time peering at me from a dark drain in one corner. I slept and chased bedbugs in my clothing to keep occupied, and three times I wolfed down the hard bread and bowl of nauseating pottage a somber jailer set at the door to my cell with a great clatter of locks and keys.

I was plotting a way to get close enough to the rat to kill it, for its presence filled me with terror every time I felt myself drifting off to sleep, when the red-haired constable and the one round as a tub—God had been as generous with him as with me—came for me.

After making our way through ever more sinister corridors, I found myself in a room similar to the first, but with certain shadowy additions in regard to company and furnishings. Behind the table, joining the man with the dark beard and robe, the scribe with the crow's beak, and the Dominicans, there was a third priest of the same order, whom the others treated with great respect and servility. Just seeing him, I was afraid. He had short gray hair cut in the shape of a helmet across his brow. His cheeks were sunken, the hands emerging from the sleeves of his habit were fleshless claws, and it was especially the fanatic, feverish gleam of eyes that seemed consumed with fever that caused me to wish never to have him as my enemy. Compared with him, the other two priests were Little Sisters of the Poor. And there was something more. At one side of the room stood a rack with ropes waiting to tear limbs from their sockets. In this room, there was nowhere for me to sit, and my legs, barely able to hold me as it was, began to tremble. A big fish was needed here for so many cats.

Again I will spare Your Mercies the details of the interminable interrogation to which I was subjected by my old acquaintances, the Dominicans, while black-robe and the new inquisitor listened and kept their silence, the constables stood like rocks behind me, and the scribe kept dipping his quill into the inkwell to note down each and every one of my answers, and my silences. This time, thanks to the participation of the new arrival—he kept passing the interrogators papers that they read attentively before posing new questions—I was able to form an idea of what I had fallen into. The horrifying word "Judaizer" was pronounced at least five times, and with each mention my hair stood on end. Those eight letters had delivered many people to the stake.

"Did you know that the blood of the de la Cruz family is not pure?"

My head reeled with those words, for I was not unaware of their sinister implication. Ever since the Jews had been expelled by the *Reyes Católicos*, King Ferdinand and Queen Isabel, the Inquisition had rigorously pursued the remnants of the Mosaic faith, particularly the *conversos* who were secretly faithful to the religion of their grandfathers. In a hypocritical Spain that gave such importance to appearances, where even the lowest of the low paraded himself as an hidalgo and old Christian, hatred of Jews was widespread, and papers, purchased or authentic, documenting one's purity of blood were indispensable if one were to obtain position or high office. And while the powerful grew rich in scandalous business dealings, shielding themselves behind masses and public charities, a violent and vengeful people killed their hunger and boredom by kissing relics, buying indulgences, and enthusiastically persecuting witches, heretics, and Judaizers. And as I once said when referring to Señor de Quevedo and others, not even the finest Spanish minds were strangers to that climate of hatred and repudiation of heterodoxy. For example, consider these words from the great Lope de Vega.

Cruel nation, which Hadrian exiled,
only to make its way to Spain,
has oppressed and defiled
our Holy Christian empire,
and with persistent barbarity
defamed the Spanish Monarchy.

Or that other great playwright, don Pedro Calderón de la Barca, who would later put these words in the mouth of one of his famous characters:

Oh, the accursed swine!
Many burned at the stake,
and it gave me such joy
to see them blaze, that I said,
as I fanned the flames,
"Heretic dogs, behold a judge
of the Holy Inquisition."

Not to forget don Francisco de Quevedo—the same Quevedo who, in the dark of night, without hesitation hastened to effect a point of honor and aid a friend of *con-*

verso blood, himself composed no few verses and lines of
prose reviling the tribe of Moses. In our day, with the
Protestants and Moors burned or exiled, the incorporation
of the Kingdom of Portugal during the reign of our good
and great Philip II had provided an abundance of secret or
public Jews into which to sink our collective teeth, and the
Inquisition kept sniffing around them like the jackal noses
out carrion. And Jews were another of the reasons that
brought the king's favorite, don Gaspar de Guzmán, the
Conde de Olivares, into a confrontation with the Supreme
Council. In his attempt to keep the vast heritage of the
Austrias intact, as he squeezed dry the exhausted purses of
vassals and threatened the selfish interests of nobles, waged
a war in Flanders, and struggled to break the backs of
Aragon and Catalonia, the Conde-Duque, as he was known,
weary of the monarchy's being held hostage to Genoese
bankers, wished to replace them with Portuguese brokers.
Their purity of blood might be in doubt, but their money
was old Christian, clean, and available to fill Spain's empty
coffers. That plan put the favorite at cross-purposes with
the councils of state, the Inquisition, and the papal nuncio
himself, while our lord and king, good-natured and extremely religious, weak in matters of conscience as in many
other things, wavered indecisively. In the end, he chose to
beat the last *maravedí* out of all his subjects rather than
contaminate the Faith.

All of which, to put it in a nutshell, was like making bread from hosts, or the other way 'round . . . however you look at it, a disaster. And as time went on, by midcentury, with the Conde de Olivares's fall from favor, the Holy Office's bill came due for collection and it unleashed one of the cruelest persecutions of converted Jews known to Spain. That was the ruin of Olivares's project, and many crucial Hispano-Portuguese bankers and suppliers took themselves off to other countries such as Holland, and with them their wealth and their commerce, to the benefit of the enemies of our crown. In other words, it all ended with our royally fucking ourselves over. And I say "ended," because between the nobles and the priests here, and the heretics there, and the whore who gave birth to them all, we bled till there was no blood left to bleed. The skinny dog gets the fleas, and we Spanish do not need anyone to ruin us; when it comes to the killing blow, we can deliver it ourselves.

So, in short, there I was, a beardless youth in the midst of all these maneuverings and machinations, and I was about to pay with my young neck. I sighed disconsolately. Then I looked toward my questioner, still the younger Dominican. The scribe was waiting, his pen poised above the paper, looking at me as if I were someone who presented every qualification for becoming good charcoal.

"I know no de la Cruz family," I replied finally, with all

the conviction I could muster. "Therefore, I have no way of knowing about the purity of their blood."

The scribe bent his head as if he had awaited that answer, his pen scratching as he performed his filthy office. The lean old priest never took his eyes from me.

"Do you know," my tormentor asked, "that Elvira de la Cruz has been accused of inciting Hebrew practices among her fellow nuns and novices?"

I swallowed. Or rather, I tried. Blood of God, I tried. But my mouth was dry as a pebble. The trap had closed, and it was a devilishly malefic one. Again I denied any knowledge, more and more afraid to hazard where all this was leading.

"Do you know that her father and brothers and other accomplices, as Judaizing as she, attempted to free her after she was discovered and confined by the chaplain and the prioress of the convent?"

Now there was an unmistakable scent of scorching meat on the air, and I was the roast. Once again, I wanted to say no, but this time I could not get the words out, and I had to shake my head. But my prosecutor, or whatever he was, did not change expression.

"And you deny that you and your fellows are a part of that Judaic conspiracy?"

At that, as frightened as I was—which was not a little— I was slightly irritated.

"I am a Basque, and an old Christian," I protested. "As good as my father, who was a soldier, and who died in the king's war."

The inquisitor gave a dismissive wave of his hand, as if every Christian died in the king's wars, and that meant nothing at all. Then the thin, till now silent, priest leaned toward the questioner, whispered a few words into his ear, and the younger man nodded respectfully. He turned toward me, and for the first time spoke. His tone was so menacing and cavernous that all at once I saw the young priest as the *non plus ultra* of understanding and sympathy.

"Repeat your name," the lean priest ordered.

"Íñ . . . Íñigo." I was so frightened by the Dominican's severe gaze, the feverish eyes sunken deep in the sockets, that I had stumbled over my own name. He continued, implacable.

"Íñigo and what more."

"Íñigo Balboa."

"And your mother's name."

"Her name is Amaya Aguirre, Reverend Father."

I had already gone through all this, it was in the papers, so the repetitions made me even more apprehensive. The priest gave me a fierce, strangely satisfied look.

"Balboa," he said, "is a Portuguese family name."

The ground seemed to drop from beneath my feet, for I did not have to be told the effect of that poisonous dart.

It was true that my surname was common on the Portuguese border, a region that my grandfather had left to enlist under the banners of the king. Suddenly—I have previously told Your Mercies that I was a bright enough lad—all the ramifications of my situation blazed with such meridional clarity that if there had been an open door I would have shot out of it like a flash.

Out of the corner of my eye, I glanced toward the rack, sitting to one side, waiting. That the Inquisition never used it as punishment but, rather, as an instrument for extracting the truth was a fact I did not find comforting. My one hope was that according to the rules of the Holy Office itself, torture could not be used against people of good reputation, royal ministers, pregnant women, servants—to make them inform against their masters—or anyone younger than fourteen . . . that is, *me*. But I was close to that fateful fourteenth, and if these men were capable of finding me Jewish ancestors, they could at their whim add the necessary months to make me eligible for their rope trick. And though the rack made men sing, it was not exactly a guitar.

"My father was not Portuguese," I protested. "He was a soldier from León, like his father, who at the end of a campaign remained in Oñate and married there. A soldier and an old Christian."

"That is what everyone says."

Then I heard the scream. It was the terrible scream of a desperate woman, muffled by distance but so piercing that it found its way along passages and corridors and through a closed door. As if they heard nothing, my inquisitors kept looking at me, unperturbed. And I shivered with fear when the lean priest shifted his eyes toward the rack and then back to me.

"How old are you?" he asked.

The scream came again, a whiplash of horror, and yet again there was no reaction from the others, as if I had been the only one who had heard. Deep in their malevolent sockets, the Dominican's fanatic eyes were two sentences of death at the stake. I trembled as if I had ague.

"Th-thirteen," I stammered.

There was an anguishing silence, broken only by the scratching of the scribe's pen. *I hope he put it down right,* I thought. *Thirteen, not one year more.*

That was when the thin priest bore in on me. His eyes gleamed even more brilliantly, with a new and unexpected glitter of scorn and loathing.

"And now," he said, "we are going to talk about Captain Alatriste."

VI. SAN GINÉS ALLEY

The gaming house was swarming with people betting their asses, even their souls. Amid the buzz of conversations and the coming and going of cardsharps and bootlickers hoping for tips, Juan Vicuña, a former sergeant of the horse guard wounded at Nieuwpoort, was crossing the room, trying to avoid spilling the Toro wine he was carrying in a jug, and looking around with satisfaction. On the half-dozen tables, cards and dice and money were changing hands, inspiring sighs, *Holy Mothers!* and flashes of naked greed. Gold and silver coins shone beneath the tallow lamps suspended from the domed brick ceiling, and business was all he could ask.

Vicuña's watering hole was in a cellar on Cava de San Miguel, very close to the Plaza Mayor; and in it, deals of every sort allowed by the mandates of our lord and king were struck, and also, as Your Mercies may have adjudged, others, scarcely concealed, that were not. The variety was as diverse as the players' imaginations, which in that day was considerable. They were playing ombre, *polla,* and one hundred—games that bled you slowly—as well as seven-up, *reparólo,* and others referred to as "quick and slick" because of the speed with which they left a man without money, speech, or breath. About them, the great Lope had written:

> *Like drawing out his sword*
> *for one who has occasion,*
> *so the game is the persuasion*
> *for one who seeks reward.*

True that only a few months before, a royal decree had been issued prohibiting gaming houses, for our fourth Philip was young, well-intentioned, and—amply aided by his pious confessor—he believed in things such as the dogma of the Virgin Mary, the Catholic cause in Europe, and the moral regeneration of his subjects in the Old and New Worlds. Forbidding gambling, like the attempt to close the bawdyhouses, however—not to mention hopes for the Catholic cause in Europe—was wishing for the sky. Because if anything besides theater, running the bulls in the plazas, and something else I will mention in good

time, impassioned Spaniards living beneath the rule of
the Austrian monarchy, it was gambling.

Towns of three thousand inhabitants wore out eighteen thousand packs of cards each year, and card games
were as often played in the streets—where sharps, cheats,
and shills improvised games in which to fleece the naive—
as they were in legal or clandestine houses, jails, brothels,
taverns, and guardposts. Important cities like Madrid and
Seville were anthills of meddlers and idlers with coins in
their purses, ready to join in around the *desencuadernada*—
the book without a binding, which was what a packet of
cards was called—or a Juan Tarafe, a name the lowlife
gave to dice games. Everyone gambled, common people
and nobility, gentlemen and rogues; even ladies, who though
they were not admitted into dens like Juan Vicuña's, were
assiduous patrons of the better gaming houses, as well
versed in clubs, trumps, and points as the next one. And as
may be expected of a violent, proud, and quick-to-draw-
steel people like we were, and are, quarrels born of a game
often ended with a "God's bones!" and a fine collection of
stab wounds.

Vicuña made it across the room, though not before
carefully eyeing some scholars of the art, which is what he
called the charlatans expert in palming and marking
cards, men who always had a winner up their sleeves,
heedful of where it fell. He also stopped to give a warm

greeting to don Raúl de la Poza, an hidalgo from a very wealthy Cuenca family, a black sheep with a taste for the spicier side of life, who was one of his best clients. A man of fixed habits, don Raúl had just arrived, as he did every night, from a brothel on Calle Francos—where he was a regular—and now would not leave until dawn, in time to attend seven-o'clock mass at San Ginés. *Escudos* were scudding across his table like sea foam on a stormy day, and always churning around him was a court of swindlers and sycophants who snuffed his candles for him, served his wine, and even brought a urinal if he was deep into the game and did not want to abandon a good hand. All in exchange for the *barato*, the *real*-or-two tip that came their way after every useful service.

That night, de la Poza was in the company of the Marqués de Abades and other friends. That made Vicuña feel easier, for it was a rare day that three or four swaggering churls were not waiting to relieve de la Poza of his winnings as he left.

Diego Alatriste thanked his host for the Toro wine, quaffing it in one long draught. He was in his shirtsleeves, unshaven, sitting on a straw mattress in the discreet room Vicuña had outfitted in his gaming house so he would have a place to retire and rest. A shutter allowed him to see into the main room without being seen himself. Boots on, sword on the taboret, loaded pistol on the blanket, *vizcaína* dagger on the pillow, and eyes sharp when from time to time he glanced through the latticed wood, it was obvious that Alatriste was on his guard. The room had a back, nearly secret, door to a passageway that emerged under an arch in the Plaza Mayor. Vicuña noted that the captain had arranged his belongings so that they could be gathered up in a quick retreat toward that door, should it be necessary. In the forty-eight hours he'd spent hiding there, Diego Alatriste had not relaxed except to nod off for forty winks. Even so, late one afternoon when Vicuña came in quietly to see if his friend needed anything, he had been met by the menacing barrel of a pistol pointed right between his eyebrows.

Alatriste did not betray his impatience by asking questions. He handed the empty jar back to Vicuña and waited, looking at him with clear, unwavering eyes whose pupils were dilated in the dim light of the oil lamp on the table.

"He will be waiting for you in a half-hour," said the old sergeant, "in San Ginés alley."

"How is he?"

"Fine. He has spent the last two days in the house of his friend the Duque de Medinaceli, and no one has bothered him. His name has not been made public, and the Law, the Inquisition, no one, is after him. The event, whatever it was, has not become public."

The captain nodded slowly, reflectively. That quiet was not strange, it was logical. The Inquisition never set bells pealing until it had the last of the loose ends well tied up. And things were still half finished. The absence of news might be part of the trap.

"What are they saying in San Felipe?"

"Rumors." Vicuña shrugged his shoulders. "That there was swordplay at La Encarnación gate, that someone died . . . They put it down more to the nuns' swains than anything else."

"Have they been to my lodgings?"

"No. But Martín Saldaña smells something. He was at the tavern. According to La Lebrijana, he said nothing specific but hinted a lot. The *corregidor*'s catchpoles are not showing themselves, he said, but there are people around watching. He did not explain who, although he mentioned *familiares* of the Holy Office. The message is simple. He is not dancing this chaconne, whatever it is, and you had better guard your hide. Apparently this is a delicate business, and it is being carried out with zeal. No one is claiming any knowledge of it."

"What do you hear of Íñigo?" The captain looked at Vicuña steadily, with no visible emotion. The veteran of

Nieuwpoort hesitated, uncomfortable. With his one hand, he kept turning the empty jug around and around.

"Nothing," he answered finally. "It's as if the earth swallowed him up."

For a moment, Alatriste sat without speaking. He stared at the wood planks between his boots and then stood up.

"Have you spoken with Dómine Pérez?"

"He is doing what he can, but it is difficult." Vicuña watched as the captain put on his rough-skinned buffcoat. "You know that the Jesuit Order and the Holy Office do not exchange confidences, and if they have the boy it may be a while before the *dómine* learns of it. As soon as he hears anything, he will tell you. He also offers you the Jesuit church, if you want safe haven. He says that the Dominicans cannot take you from there, not even if they swear you killed the papal nuncio." He glanced through the lattice toward the gaming room, and then looked back toward the captain. "And whatever it is you've done, Diego, I hope to God you have not actually killed the nuncio."

Alatriste asked for his sword and slid it into its scabbard. He cinched it on, and then stuck his flintlock pistol into his belt, after pulling back the hammer to be sure it was well oiled.

"I will tell you about it another time," he said.

He prepared to leave as he had come, without explanation and without thanks. In the world that he and the veteran sergeant of the horse guard shared, these terms of the arrangement were understood.

Vicuña laughed a loud, soldier's laugh. "By all that's holy, Diego. I am your friend, but I am not curious. Besides, I would hate to die of noose poisoning. So it would be best if you never tell me."

It was deepest night when, with his cape tight around him and hat pulled low, the captain emerged beneath the dark arcades of the Plaza Mayor and walked the short distant toward Calle Nueva. No one among the few stragglers out and about paid any attention to him, except for a lady of the night who when she met him between two arches offered, without much enthusiasm, to reduce his weight by twelve *cuarto* coins. He crossed through the Guadalajara gate, where a pair of guards were dozing before the closed window shutters of the silver shops, and then, to avoid the constables who tended to station themselves in that area, went down Calle de las Hileras to El Arenal. Finally, he again turned up the hill toward San Ginés alley, where at that hour refugees from the law were wont to gather in the cool night air.

As Your Mercies know, the churches of the period were havens of asylum, where no ordinary law could reach. So anyone who stole, wounded, or killed—all the things they called being "about their work"—could take sanctuary in a church or convent, where the priests, highly jealous of their privileges, would defend him tooth and nail from the royal authorities. So popular was it to plead innocent and seek protection that some of the principal churches were chock-a-block with clients enjoying the sanctity of their refuge. In those crowded communities, one tended to find the cream of society; there was not enough rope to do honor to their genteel gullets. Because of his profession, Diego Alatriste himself had once had to recur to that practice. Even don Francisco de Quevedo, in his youth, had found himself in similar, if not worse, straits when in Venice, he and the Duque de Osuna staged a coup and he had had to escape disguised as a beggar.

The fact is that places such as Los Naranjos courtyard of the Seville cathedral, for example, or a good dozen places in Madrid, among them San Ginés, had gained the dubious privilege of taking in the flower of the city's braggarts, cutthroats, thieves, and carousers. And all this illustrious brotherhood, which after all had to eat, drink, satisfy its needs, and conduct its personal business, took advantage of the night hours to take a walk, commit new villainy, settle accounts, or whatever opportunity presented itself. These felons also received their friends there, even their whores and cronies, so that by night the area around these churches—even church buildings themselves—became

the criminals' tavern, even their brothel. There, real or invented feats were aired, death sentences were carried out
by hired steel, and there, too, throbbed the colorful and ferocious pulse of the dangerous underbelly of Spain: the
world of scoundrels, thieves, and other caballeros of the
low life, men whose portraits never hung on the walls of
palaces but whose existence was recorded in immortal
pages. Some of which—and not the worst, certainly—
were written by don Francisco.

> *Mercilessly, they tortured Grullo,*
> *who, with the truth at the end of a rope,*
> *said, "It wasn't me"—the defense*
> *of rack and wedding day: No hope.*

Or this very celebrated one:

> *In the house of rogues*
> *at the foot of the gallows,*
> *for being the cutpurse I was*
> *they sent me into shadows.*

San Ginés alley was one of the favorite sites of these
refugees, and at night when they came out to get a breath
of air, the alley came to life and temporary stalls were set
up to satisfy the fly-by-nights' hunger. It was a dignified

assembly that evaporated as if by incantation as soon as a constable showed his face.

When Diego Alatriste arrived, there were some thirty souls in the narrow alleyway: bullies, petty thieves, a few whores settling accounts with their customers, and idlers and rabble standing around talking or drinking cheap wine from wineskins and demijohns. There was very little light—only a small lantern hanging beneath an arch at the corner of the alley. That area was almost entirely in shadow, and more than half the people present were swathed in their cloaks, so that the atmosphere, although lively with conversation, was tenebrous; entirely appropriate for the kind of appointment that brought the captain there. It was also a place where someone overly curious and inquisitive, or perhaps a constable—if he was not with a patrol and well armed—might in the blink of a "Jesus God!" find it permanently difficult to swallow.

The captain recognized don Francisco de Quevedo despite the collar drawn across his face, and casually made his way toward him. The two of them drifted off to one side, away from the lantern where the poet had been standing, cape collars up and hat brims down to the eyebrows, a look very much in style among the men in the alley.

"My friends have made inquiries," the poet reported after their first exchange of impressions. "It seems certain that don Vicente and his sons were being watched by the

Inquisition. And it smells to me as if someone seized the occasion to kill several birds with one stone. Including you, Captain."

Then in a low voice, turning away from anyone passing by, don Francisco brought Alatriste up-to-date on everything he had been able to find out. The Holy Office, persistent and patient, very well informed by its spies regarding the de la Cruz family's intentions, had let them proceed, hoping to catch them *in flagrante*. The Inquisition's intent had not been to defend Padre Coroado, just the opposite. Now that he was under the protection of the Conde de Olivares, with whom the Inquisition was waging an undeclared war, they hoped that the scandal would discredit both the convent and its protector. In the process, they would also seize a family of *conversos*; a burning at the stake never harmed the prestige of the Supreme Council. The problem was that they had been unable to snatch anyone alive. Don Vicente de la Cruz and his younger son, don Luis, had paid a high price, dying in the ambush. The older son, don Jerónimo, although badly wounded, had escaped and was in hiding.

"And what about us?" asked Alatriste.

Light glanced off the poet's glasses as he shook his head. "No names have been revealed. It was so dark that no one recognized us. And anyone who was near enough to recognize us is in no condition to tell."

"Nevertheless, they know that we were involved."

"They may." Don Francisco made a vague gesture. "But they have no legal proof. As for me, I am beginning once again to bask in the favor of the king and the king's favorite, Olivares, and as long as I am not caught with my hands in the dough, it will be difficult to do anything to me." He paused, preoccupied. "As for you, my friend, I do not know what to say. They hope to find something that will indicate your guilt. Or they may be quietly looking for you."

Two ruffians and a prostitute walked by, arguing heatedly, and don Francisco and the captain moved out of their way, closer to the wall.

"And what has happened to Elvira de la Cruz?"

The poet sighed despondently. "Arrested. The poor girl will bear the worst of it. She is in the secret dungeons in Toledo, and I fear that there will be a burning."

"And Íñigo?"

The pause stretched into silence. Alatriste's voice had sounded cool, and void of emotion. He had left me for last. Don Francisco glanced around at the people chatting and strolling in the shadows of the alleyway. He turned to his friend.

"He, too, is in Toledo." He fell silent, and shook his head with a gesture of impotence. "They caught him near the convent."

Alatriste said nothing for a long while, watching the movement around him. From the nearby corner came the notes of a guitar.

"He is only a boy," he said finally. "We must get him out of there."

"Impossible. You should put your energies toward not joining him there. I imagine that they are counting on his testimony to incriminate us."

"They would not dare mistreat him."

Behind the heavy collar, don Francisco laughed his sour, mirthless laugh. "The Inquisition, Captain, dares all things."

"Then we have to do something."

He said it very coldly, obstinately, his eyes focused on the end of the passageway, where the guitar continued to play. Don Francisco looked in the same direction.

"I agree," the poet put in. "But know not what."

"You have friends at court."

"I have marshaled them all. I have not forgotten that it was I who got you into this."

The captain raised a listless hand, brushing away don Francisco's guilt. It was reasonable that as a friend he expected the poet to do anything in his power to help; it was another matter to blame him for anything. Alatriste had collected his purse for the job, and I was, after all, *his* responsibility. He was silent for so long that the poet looked at him uneasily.

"Do not think of turning yourself in," he murmured. "That would help no one, least of all yourself."

Still Alatriste did not speak. Three or four of the refugees from justice had begun chatting nearby, with a lot of "ol' frens," "ol' cumr'd," "fine cab'lleros we"—things none of them had ever been in danger of being. They were tossing names around, fast and furious. Hellion, Devilspawn, Maniferro—a man with a hand of iron and famous in the world of Cervantes's master criminal Monipodio. Then the captain did speak.

"Earlier," he said in a low voice, "you said that the Inquisition wanted to get several birds with one stone. What more do you know of that?"

Don Francisco answered in the same low tone. "You. You were the fourth winged target, but they were only partly successful. The whole scheme was cooked up, it seems, by two close acquaintances of yours: Luis de Alquézar and Fray Emilio Bocanegra."

"'Sblood!"

The poet paused, believing that the captain was going to add something to his oath, but he had nothing more to offer. He was still facing the alley, motionless behind the shelter of his cape and the hat that hid his features.

"Apparently," don Francisco continued, "they have not forgiven you that business of the Prince of Wales and Buck-ingham. And now they find a golden opportunity: Padre Coroado, the convent of the king's favorite, the family of *conversos,* and you yourself. What a pretty package that would make for an *auto-da-fé.*"

Don Francisco was interrupted by one of the ruffians, who bumped into him as he leaned back to drink from a wineskin. He turned with a great clatter of the iron at his belt, and with a very churlish attitude.

"God's bodkins! I fear you have discommoded me, *compañero!*"

The poet looked at him with contempt, and stepped back. With heavy irony he recited under his breath,

You, Bernardo among the French
and amid Spaniards, Roland. Marry!
Your sword is as lethal as Galen,
and your face an apothecary.

The swaggerer heard him, however, and made a great show of demanding redress.

"God's bones!" he said. "None of this Galen, or Roland, or Bernardo. I have a perfectly good name, which is Antón Novillo de la Gamella! And I am a person of worth, with the necessary tools to slice off the ears of anyone who would crowd me!"

As he spoke, he fumbled conspicuously with his weapon, though he decided not to draw it until he was sure of his cards. About that time his companions stepped up beside him, also itching for a fight, planting their feet wide apart with great sword clankings and mustache twistings. They were the sort who so prided themselves on being cocks that to hear themselves crow they would confess to things they had never done. Among them they could have knifed a one-armed man in a breath, but that man was not don Francisco. Alatriste watched the poet pull his dagger from the back of his belt and gather his heavy cape to protect his torso. Alatriste was preparing to do the same—castanets were setting the rhythm for a lively dance—when one of the swaggerer's comrades, a mountain of a man wearing a huntsman's cap and a baldric a hand-width's wide across his chest to support an enormous sword, said: "Two hundred slices off these señores, comrades. Here, men do not live to a ripe old age, but are picked green."

He had more pips and pocks on his face than a music score, and he had the accent and look of the ruffians that hang around del Potro plaza in Córdoba—*Valencian whore, Cordovan rogue*, was the old saying—and he, too, was making a move toward lightening his scabbard, though he did not carry it through. He was waiting for yet one more colleague to join them, for even though they were four against two, he still did not seem to feel it was an even match.

Then, to everyone's surprise, Diego Alatriste burst out laughing.

"Here, now, Cagafuego," he said, with festive sarcasm. "Grant us some slack. Do not kill this caballero and me outright, only a little at a time. For old times' sake."

Stupefied, the hulking brute stood staring at Alatriste, abashed, trying in the black of night to recognize the speaker in the dark cloak. Finally, he scratched his brow beneath the cap he wore pulled down to eyebrows so thick they seemed one straight line.

"By our Blessed Virgin," he murmured finally. "If it's not Captain Alatriste."

"The same," he replied. "The last time we met it was in the shadow of a cell."

The reference to that "last time" was accurate. The captain had been sent to the city prison for debts, where as his first bit of business he had held a slaughterer's knife to the throat of this Cagafuego named Bartolo, who passed as the toughest among the prisoners. That had confirmed Diego Alatriste's reputation as a man with something substantial between his legs, along with the respect of Cagafuego and the other prisoners. A respect he turned to loyalty when he shared with them the stews and bottles of wine Caridad la Lebrijana and his friends sent to comfort his stay in his inhospitable lodgings. Even after he was free, Alatriste had continued to offer a helping hand from time to time.

"You were clubbing sardines for a while, were you not, Señor Cagafuego? At least, if I remember correctly, that is where you were heading."

The attitude of Cagafuego's companions had changed—including Antón Novillo de la Gamella's—and now they were listening with professional curiosity and a certain consideration, as if the deference their friend in crime showed this cloaked man was a better recommendation than a papal brief. As for Cagafuego, he seemed pleased that Alatriste was so well informed about his recent honors.

"Why, yes, Captain, that is indeed so," he replied, and his tone had warmed considerably from that of the two hundred slices promised shortly before. "And I would still be there in the king's galleys as strokesman, hands to oars, rowing to the music of the shackles and whips, were it not for my saint, Blasa Pizorra. She services a scribe, and between the two of them, they softened up the judge."

"And why are you here now? Or are you visiting?"

"Seeking refuge, by my faith, refuge," he lamented, not without resignation. "For three days ago, we—I and my comrades here—in good Catalan fashion separated the soul from a catchpole and fled here to the church until everything blows over. Or until my fine bawd can scrape together a few ducats. For as you know, YerM'cy, the only justice is the justice you buy."

"I am happy to see you."

In the darkness, Bartolo Cagafuego's lips turned upward in something resembling a huge, friendly smile.

"And I am happy to see YerM'cy looking so well. 'Pon my oath, I am at your service here in San Ginés, no lily livers here, and I bring this good ventilator"—he patted his sword, which clinked against dagger and poniards— "to serve God and my comrades, and to carve a few holes in someone these early morning hours, should we need to."

He looked toward Quevedo with a conciliatory nod, and turned back to the captain, touching two fingers to his cap. "And forgive the error."

Two trollops came running by, holding up their petticoats as they ran. The guitar at the corner stopped in midchord, and a wave of uneasiness stirred the rabble in the alley. Everyone turned to look.

"The Law! The Law!" someone shouted.

From around the corner came the hue and cry of constables and catchpoles. There were shouts of "Hold there!" and "I said *Hold there*, by God," and then came the well-known warnings of "In the name of the King." The pale light of the lantern was doused as the parishioners scattered at lightning speed: the refugees into the church and the rest emptying the alley and Calle Mayor. And in less time than it takes to dispatch a soul, there was not a shadow left behind.

Diego Alatriste retraced his steps down Cava de San Miguel and made a broad circle around the Plaza Mayor to reach the Tavern of the Turk. Standing motionless on the opposite side of the street for a long while, hidden in darkness, he observed the closed shutters and lighted window on the second floor where Caridad la Lebrijana made her home. She was awake, or at least she had left a light on as a signal for him. *I am here and I am waiting for you,* the message seemed to say.

But the captain did not cross the street. Instead he waited quietly, still masked by his cape, his hat pulled low, attempting to blend into the shadows of the arcade. Calle Toledo and the corner of Calle Arcabuz were deserted, but it was impossible to know whether someone might be secretly watching from the shelter of a doorway. All he could see was the empty street and that lighted window, where he thought he saw a shadow. Perhaps La Lebrijana was awake, waiting for him. He imagined her moving about the room, with the cord of her nightdress loose across her naked, dark-skinned shoulders, and he longed for the scent of that body which, despite the many wars it had fought in other days, mercenary battles, strange hands and kisses, was still beautiful, firm, and warm, as comforting as sleep, or oblivion.

Guided by his instinct of self-preservation, he fought the desire to cross the street and bury himself in that welcoming flesh. His hand brushed the grip of the *vizcaína* dagger he wore over his left kidney, close to his sword, a counterweight to the pistol hidden by his cape. Again, ever cautious, he searched for the dark form of an enemy shadow. And he longed to find one.

Ever since he had learned that I was in the hands of the Inquisition, and had also learned the identity of the ones who had pulled the strings of the ambush, he had harbored a lucid, icy rage bordering on desperation, and he needed somehow to purge it. The fate of don Vicente de la Cruz and his sons, and that of the now-imprisoned novice, had become secondary. In the rules of the dangerous game in which he often pawned his own skin, that was part of the deal. In every combat there were losses and gains, and the game of life provided the same ups and downs. He assumed that from the beginning, with his usual impassivity: an acceptance that at times seemed to be indifference, but was in fact nothing other than the stoic resignation of an old soldier.

But with me it was different, if Your Mercies will allow me to find a way to say this. To Diego Alatriste y Tenorio, veteran of the *tercios* of Flanders and those rough and dangerous times, I represented the word "remorse." It was not easy to coolly assign me to the list of "downs" resulting from a bad adventure or assault. I was his responsibility, whether he liked it or not. And just as one does not choose his friends or his women, but is instead chosen by them, life, my dead father, fate, had set me in his path. There was no way he could close his eyes to an unpleasant truth: I made him vulnerable. In the life he had chosen to live, Diego Alatriste was as much a whoreson as the next; but he was a whoreson who played according to certain rules. For that reason he was quiet, and kept to himself, which was as good a way as any other to be desperate.

And that was why he was peering into the dark shadows of the street, hoping to spot a constable lurking there, a spy, any enemy at all that he could use to calm the sensation that was griping his bowels and making him clench his teeth until his jaw hurt. He wanted to find someone and then slip toward him in the darkness, without a sound, press him against the wall, gag him with his cape, and without a single word drive his dagger into his throat until he stopped moving and the Devil took him.

Because if we are considering rules, those happened to be his.

VII. MEN OF ONE BOOK

God never deserts crows or rooks, not even notaries. And he did not completely desert me. For, believe it or not, I was not tortured unbearably. The Holy Office had its rules, too, and despite their cruelty and fanaticism, some of them were observed to the letter. I received my share of slapping and lashes, I cannot deny. And no few privations and rough interrogations. But once they confirmed my age, those not-yet-lived fourteen years kept at a safe distance the contraption of wood, rope, and wheels that at every questioning I could see in the far corner of the room. Even the beatings they gave me were limited in number, intensity, and duration.

Others, however, were not as lucky. I do not know whether the woman's scream I had heard on my first day had come with or without the help of the rack. If the latter, unfortunately, she had been installed upon it, her limbs pulled with turn after turn of the wheel, until her bones were cracked from their sockets. I continued to hear screams frequently, until suddenly, they ceased. That was the same day I found myself again in the interrogation room and finally met the unfortunate Elvira de la Cruz.

She was small and plump, and in no way resembled the romanticized vision I had concocted in my mind. But no matter, not even the most perfect beauty could have offset that mercilessly shaved head, those red-rimmed eyes sunken in dark circles of insomnia and suffering, and, beneath the filthy serge of her habit, the bruises of cuffs around her wrists and ankles. She was sitting down—soon I learned that she was unable to stand without help—and her gaze was the most vacant and desolate I had ever seen: an absolute emptiness born of the pain and exhaustion and bitterness of one who knows the depths of the darkest pit ever imagined. She must have been about eighteen or nineteen years old, but she looked like a decrepit old woman. If she shifted slightly in her chair, it was slowly and painfully, as if her joints were all crippled. And sadly, that was exactly what had happened.

As for me, although it is not a sign of good breeding to boast, they had not torn from me a single one of the answers they wanted. Not even when one of the torturers, the redheaded one, took on the task of measuring every

inch of my back with a bull's pizzle. But although I was
covered with welts and had to sleep on my stomach—if
that agonizing and restless state somewhere between real-
ity and the ghosts of imagination can be called sleep—
they did not get one word from dry, cracked lips now crusted
with blood that was mine, not poor de la Cruz's. No words,
that is, other than groans of pain or protests of innocence.
*That night I was returning home alone. My master, Captain
Alatriste, was nowhere around. I have never heard anything
about the de la Cruz family. I am an old Christian, and my
father died for the king in Flanders.* . . . And then I would
start from the beginning again. *That night I was returning
home* . . .

There was no mercy in them, not even those specks of
humanity that can occasionally be glimpsed in the most
heartless of souls. Priests, judge, scribe, and torturers acted
with such rigorous coldness and distance that that was precisely what evoked the most horror. Even more bloodcurdling than the suffering they were capable of inflicting
was the icy determination of those who *know* they are
backed by divine and human laws and who at no moment
doubt the righteousness of what they are doing.

Later, with time, I learned that although all men are
capable of good and evil, the worst among them are those
who, when they commit evil, do so by shielding themselves in the authority of others, in their subordination, or

in the excuse of following orders. And even worse are those who believe they are justified by their God. Because in the secret dungeons of Toledo, nearly at the cost of my life, I learned that there is nothing more despicable or more dangerous than the malevolent individual who goes to sleep every night with a clear conscience. That is true evil. Especially when paired with ignorance, superstition, stupidity, or power, all of which often travel together.

And worst of all is the person who acts as exegete of The Word—whether it be from the Talmud, the Bible, the Koran, or any other book already written or yet to come. I am not fond of giving advice—no one can pound opinions into another's head—but here is a piece that costs you nothing: Never trust a man who reads only one book.

I do not know what books those men had read, but as for consciences, I am sure they slept soundly. Though now that they are all in Hell, where it is to be hoped they burn throughout eternity, they will never sleep again. By that point in my Calvary, I had learned the name of the one who played the lead role, the somber and fleshless priest with the feverish eyes. He was Fray Emilio Bocanegra, president of the Council of Six Judges, the most feared tribunal of the Holy Office. Also, according to what I heard Captain Alatriste and his friends say, he was one of my

master's most relentless enemies. He had been the one setting the course of the interrogations, and now the other
priests and the silent judge in the black robe acted as mere
witnesses, while the scribe set down the Dominican's questions and my laconic replies.

But this time was different, for when I came before
them they did not ask me questions but addressed them to
poor Elvira de la Cruz. And I sensed things were taking a
disturbing turn when I saw Fray Emilio point to me.

"Do you know that young man?"

My apprehension turned to panic—unlike Elvira, I had
not as yet reached my limits—when the novice nodded
her shorn head without even looking my way. Alarmed, I
saw the scribe waiting, quill poised, his eyes on Elvira de la
Cruz and the inquisitor.

"Answer with words," ordered Fray Emilio.

The unhappy girl breathed a scarcely audible "Yes."
The scribe dipped the quill into the inkwell and wrote,
and more than ever in my life, I felt the ground yawning
beneath my feet.

"Do you know if he observes any Jewish practices?"

The second "Yes" from Elvira de la Cruz made me
jump up with a cry of protest, silenced by a hard thump on
the nape of my neck. It came courtesy of the redheaded
man who had become the one in charge of anything having to do with me; they may have feared that the larger

man would silence me with one blow of his fist. Indifferent to my protest, Fray Emilio pointed toward me, though he never took his eyes from the girl.

"Do you reiterate before this Holy Tribunal that the one called Íñigo Balboa has manifest Hebraic beliefs in word and deed, and that he, along with your father, brother, and other accomplices, participated in the conspiracy to take you from your convent?"

The third "Yes" was more than I could take. I pulled away from the redheaded guard and shouted that the poor girl was lying and that I had never had anything to do with the Jewish religion. Then to my surprise, instead of ignoring me as he had previously, Fray Emilio turned to me with a smile. It was a smile of triumphant loathing, so frightening and vicious that it nailed me to the spot, mute, immobilized, breathless. Delighting in every moment, the Dominican went to the table where the others were seated and picked up the chain and amulet Angélica de Alquézar had given me at the Acero fountain. He showed it to me, then to the members of the tribunal, and last to the novice.

"And have you seen this magic seal before? This amulet is tied to the horrendous superstition of Hebraic cabala, and was taken from the aforesaid Íñigo Balboa at the time of his arrest by *familiares* of the Holy Office. It is proof of his involvement in this Jewish conspiracy."

Elvira de la Cruz had never once looked at me. Neither did she now look at Angélica's charm, which Fray Emilio was holding before her eyes. She merely repeated the same "Yes," her eyes to the ground, so broken that she did not even seem shamed. Weary, uncaring, as if all she wished for was to have everything over with, so she could throw herself into a corner and sleep the sleep of which she had been deprived half her life.

As for me, I was so terrified I could not even protest. The rack no longer worried me. Now my urgent preoccupation was to learn whether or not they burned boys younger than fourteen at the stake.

"Confirmed. It has Alquézar's signature."

Álvaro de la Marca, Conde de Guadalmedina, was wearing a suit of fine green wool trimmed with silver, suede boots, and an elaborate Flemish lace collar. He had fair skin, fine hands, and was quite handsome, and he did not lose a whit of his elegance—it was said that he cut the finest figure at court—even though he was straddling a taboret in the small, dingy room in Juan Vicuña's gaming house. On the other side of the lattice, the main room was crowded with gamblers. The count had played for a bit, with little luck, for his mind was not on the cards, then, using the excuse of a call of nature, he left and came to the back room. There he had met Captain Alatriste and don Francisco de Quevedo, who, unrecognizable in their capes, had come by way of the secret door in the Plaza Mayor.

"And Your Mercies hit the mark," Guadalmedina continued. "The objective was, in fact, to effect a bloodless coup against Olivares by discrediting the convent. And, in passing, seize the opportunity to settle accounts with Alatriste. They have fabricated a tale of a Jewish conspiracy, and intend to use the stake."

"The boy, too?" asked don Francisco.

The poet's somber black clothing—the one note of color, as always, the cross of Santiago on his breast—contrasted with the aristocrat's affected elegance. The poet was sitting beside the captain, cape doubled across his shoulder, sword at his waist, hat upon his knees. When Álvaro de la Marca heard his question, he busied himself filling a glass with the muscatel from the jug on a second taboret, which also held a clay pipe and a pouch of shredded tobacco. The muscatel was from Málaga, and the jar was already half empty because Quevedo had given it his attention the minute he came in the door, sour as always, cursing the night, the street, and his thirst.

"Him, as well," the aristocrat confirmed. "The novice and the boy are all they have, because the other surviving member of the family, the elder son, cannot be found." He shrugged his shoulders and paused, his expression grave. "According to what I've been told, they are preparing an *auto-da-fé* for the highest-level prisoners."

"You are sure of that, Your Mercy?"

"Absolutely. I have pushed everywhere possible, paying good coin. As our friend Alatriste here would say, to score a counterstrike, it takes a lot of gunpowder. There is money enough, but in dealing with the Inquisition, even venality has its limits."

The captain was mute. He was sitting on the cot, doublet unfastened, slowly rubbing a whetstone along the edge of his dagger. The light from the oil lamp left his eyes in shadow.

"I am amazed that Alquézar is reaching so high," offered don Francisco, cleaning his eyeglasses on the tail of his doublet. "It is extremely bold of a royal secretary to take on the king's favorite, even if there is another hand in the works."

Guadalmedina took a few sips of muscatel and clicked his tongue, frowning. Then he dabbed at his curly mustache with a perfumed handkerchief he pulled from his sleeve.

"You should not be surprised. In recent months, Alquézar has gained great influence among those close to the king. He is the creature of the Council of Aragon, for whose members he performs important services, and only lately he has bought several councilors from Castile. Furthermore, through the influence of Fray Emilio Bocanegra, he enjoys support among fanatical members of the Holy Office. Around Olivares, he continues to be submissive, but it is obvious that he is playing his own game. With every day that passes, he grows stronger, and adds to his fortune."

"Where is he getting his money?" the poet asked.

Álvaro de la Marca shrugged again. He had filled his pipe and was lighting it from a candle. Pipe and tobacco also entertained Juan Vicuña, who liked to smoke when he was passing time with Diego Alatriste. But despite its well-known curative properties—it had the apothecary Fadrique's strong recommendation—the captain was not taken with the aromatic leaf brought on the galleons from the Indies. As for Quevedo, he preferred snuff.

"No one knows," said the count, blowing smoke through his nostrils. "Perhaps Alquézar works for someone other than himself. What we do know is that he manages gold like a magician, and he is corrupting everything he touches. Including Olivares, who could have sent him packing back to Huesca months ago, but who now treats him rather gingerly. They say that the royal secretary aspires to be protonotary of Aragon, even minister of foreign relations. If he achieves that, he will be untouchable."

Diego Alatriste appeared not to be listening. He set his whetstone on the straw mattress and ran one finger along the edge of the blade. Then, very slowly, he reached for the sheath and put the *vizcaína* back in it. Only then did he look at Guadalmedina.

"Is there no way to help Íñigo?"

Through blowing smoke, the captain could see the count's friendly but pained smile.

"I fear not. You know as well as I that to fall into the hands of the Inquisition is to be caught in an efficient and implacable machine." He frowned, pensively stroking his goatee. "The thing that amazes me is that they have not arrested you."

"I am in hiding."

"That is not what I mean. They have ways of finding out what they want to know. . . . Equally strange is that they have not come to your house. That means they do not as yet have evidence against you."

"They could care less about evidence," said don Francisco, taking possession of the jug of muscatel. "They fabricate it or they buy it. Money, after all," and between sips, he recited,

"Can buy honor, and take it away,
break any law, destroy any prey."

Guadalmedina, who was lifting his pipe to his mouth, stopped in midair.

"No, with your pardon, Señor de Quevedo. The Holy

Office is very punctilious, according to the circumstance.
If there is no proof, no matter how fervently Bocanegra
swears that the captain is in it up to his neck, the Council
will not approve any action against him. And if they have
nothing official, it is because the boy has not talked."

"They always talk." The poet took a long swallow, and
then another. "And besides, he is still a boy."

"Well, by my faith, I say he has not spoken, however
young he may be. That is what I understand from the persons with whom I have consulted all day. I assure you, Alatriste, that with the gold I squandered today in your service,
we could have peacefully settled that matter of the Kerken-
nahs. There are things that can be bought with gold."

And Álvaro Luis Gonzaga de la Marca y Álvarez de
Sidonia, Conde de Guadalmedina, grandee of Spain, confidant of our lord and king, admired of all the ladies at
court and envied by no few caballeros of the finest breeding, gave the hired sword a look of sincere friendship.

"Did you bring what I asked of you?" asked Alatriste.

The count's smile widened. "I did." He set his pipe
aside, and pulled from his waistcoat a small packet, which
he handed to the captain. "Here you have it."

Someone less knowledgeable than don Francisco de
Quevedo would have been surprised at the familiarity between the aristocrat and the veteran. It was widely known
that the count had more than once counted on Diego Ala-

triste's blade to resolve matters that required a steady hand
and few scruples, such as the death of the troublesome
Marqués de Soto, and another, similar, problem. But that
did not mean that the one who pays owes anything to the
one he has hired, much less that a grandee of Spain, who
had considerable influence at court, would meddle in the
affairs of the Inquisition on behalf of a don Nobody whose
sword he could have bought by merely rattling his purse.
But as Señor de Quevedo knew very well, there was more
between Diego Alatriste and Álvaro de la Marca than
their dark business dealings.

Nearly ten years before, Guadalmedina had been a
naive young blood serving on the galleys of the viceroys of
Naples and Sicily. He had found himself in difficulty on
that disastrous day in the Kerkennah Islands when Moors
attacked the troops of the Catholic king as they waded
through the shallow bay. The Duque de Nocera, with whom
don Álvaro was serving, had suffered five terrible wounds
when they were beset on every side by the Arabs' curved-
blade *saif*s, pikes, and harquebuses. The Spanish were being killed man by man; they were no longer fighting for
the king but in defense of their own lives, killing in order
not to die, in a horrifying retreat through water up to their
waists. It had become, as Guadalmedina told it, a question
of dining that night either in Constantinople or with Christ.
A Moor stood in his way, and he lost his sword as he ran

him through, so the man behind him struck twice with his *saif* as de la Marca whirled around looking for his dagger in the water.

He was picturing himself dead, or a slave—more the former than the latter—when a few soldiers who were holding out in a group and firing themselves up by shouting "Spain! Spain! All for Spain!" heard his cries for help over the roar of harquebus fire. Two or three came to his aid, splashing through the mud and knifing Arabs right and left. One of the rescuers was a soldier with an enormous mustache and gray-green eyes, who, after slashing a Moor's face with his pike, put one arm around young Guadalmedina's shoulders and dragged him through mud red with blood toward the boats and galleys anchored near the beach. Once there, they still had to battle, with Guadalmedina bleeding on the sand amid flying shot and arrows and flashing blades, until the soldier with the light eyes could finally pull the injured man into the water, load him onto his back, and carry him to the skiff of the last galley. Behind them they could hear the yells of the poor wretches who had not escaped, but were murdered or captured for slaves on that fateful beach.

Guadalmedina was looking into those same eyes now, in Juan Vicuña's little room. And—as sometimes happens, but always in generous souls—throughout the years that had passed since that bloody day, Álvaro de la Marca had not forgotten his debt. And the debt was even greater when he learned that the soldier to whom he owed his life——the one whose comrades called him captain out of respect, though he had not earned that rank——had fought in Flanders under the banners of his father, Conde Fernando de la Marca. It was a debt, however, that Diego Alatriste never called due except in extreme cases, such as the recent adventure of the two Englishmen. And now, when my life was at stake.

"Returning to our Íñigo," Guadalmedina continued, "if he does not testify against you, Alatriste, the matter stops there. But he is in custody, and seemingly they expect him to incriminate you. Which makes him a prize prisoner of the Inquisition."

"What can they do to him?"

"They can do anything. They are going to burn the girl at the stake, as sure as Christ is God. As for him, it depends. He could be freed after a few years in prison, after two hundred lashes, or after being made to wear the cone hat of infidels . . . or who knows what? But the risk of the stake is real."

"And what about Olivares?" don Francisco put in.

Guadalmedina made a vague gesture. He had recovered his pipe and was puffing on it, eyes half closed against the smoke.

"He has received the message and will consider the matter, although we must not expect too much from him. If he has something to say, he will let us know."

"*Pardiez!* This is not a minor matter," don Francisco grumbled.

Guadalmedina turned to the poet with a faint frown. "His Majesty's favorite has other matters to attend to."

He said it rather tartly. Álvaro de la Marca admired the poet's talent, and respected him as the captain's friend. They also had friends in common—both had been in Naples with the Duque de Osuna. But the aristocrat was a poet himself in moments of leisure, and it smarted when he thought that this Señor de la Torre de Juan Abad did not appreciate his verses. And still more that Quevedo had been unimpressed when in hopes of winning his approval, Guadalmedina had dedicated a poem to him that was one of the best to come from his quill, the well-known lines that begin,

Behind good Roch, lame supplicant . . .

The captain was paying no attention to them, intent on unwrapping the packet the aristocrat had brought. Álvaro de la Marca, puffing his pipe, watched closely.

"Use them with caution, Alatriste," he said finally.

The captain did not reply. He was examining the objects Guadalmedina had brought. On the wrinkled blanket lay a map and two keys.

The cauldron of the Prado gardens was boiling. It was the evening *rúa*, the time of the stylized social parade. Carriages driving from the Guadalajara gate and the Calle Mayor tarried between the fountains and beneath the poplar groves as the setting sun painted the roof tiles of Madrid. The area from the corner of Calle Alcalá to San Jerónimo road was a mass of covered and open coaches, cavaliers who had checked their horses to chat with the ladies, duennas in their nunlike white headgear, aproned servant girls, pages, hawkers selling Caño Dorado water and mead, and women peddling fruit, small pots of custard, jars of conserves, and sweets.

As a grandee of Spain with the right to wear his hat in the presence of our lord and king, the Conde de Guadalmedina was also entitled to drive a coach with four mules; the team of six was reserved for His Majesty. However, on this occasion, which required discretion, he had chosen from his coach house a modest carriage without visible insignia, drawn by two modest gray mules and driven by a servant without livery. It was large enough, however, that the count, don Francisco de Quevedo, and Captain Alatriste could fit comfortably as they drove up and down the

Prado, awaiting the arranged meeting. They passed unnoticed among the dozens of coaches moving slowly at that twilight hour when all Madrid paraded in the proximity of the convent of the Hieronymites: grave canons taking their constitutionals to whet an appetite for dinner; students as rich in wit as poor in *maravedís*; merchants and artisans with swords at their belts, proclaiming themselves to be grand hidalgos; and especially, swarms of young swains strumming guitars as if caressing feminine curves; pale hands fastening and unfastening carriage curtains; and many a lady, veiled or not, revealing outside the footboard of her coach, as if accidentally, a froth of seductive petticoat.

As the day languished, the Prado filled with shadows; and as reputable people left, they were replaced by hussies, caballeros in search of adventure, and rogues in general, the park becoming a stage for quarrels, amorous rendezvous, and furtive consultations beneath the trees. This scene was permeated with stealth and good manners: notes exchanged from coach to coach, accompanied by torrid glances, fluttering fans, insinuations, and promises. Some of the more respectable caballeros and damas who met there with the pretense of not knowing one another were plotting an assignation as soon as the sun set, using the intimacy of a coach, or the shelter of one of the stone fountains that adorned the walk, to claim a prize. And there

were the usual altercations, stabbings involving jealous
lovers or husbands who had found new spices in the pot.
It was upon the latter theme that the deceased Conde de
Villamediana—dead, it was said, because his tongue was
too loose, his innards strung across the Calle Mayor right
in the middle of the *rúa*—had written these celebrated
verses:

In Madrid I do not go to the Prado,
for as much as it is praised
I know that its welcoming meadows
are already overgrazed.

Álvaro de la Marca, a wealthy bachelor and habitué of
the Prado and Calle Mayor, and therefore one of those
who in Madrid produced cuckolds in riatas of a dozen, was
singing in a different register that evening. Dressed in a
discreet woolen as gray as his coach and mules, he was trying not to attract attention. As he peered through the coach's
drawn curtains, he would quickly draw back at the glimpse
of an open coach bearing ladies copiously adorned with
silver passementerie, silk, and ruffles from Naples, women
he did not wish to greet and to whom he was better known
than was convenient. At the other window, don Francisco
de Quevedo was also observing from behind a half-closed
curtain. Diego Alatriste sat between them, legs in long

leather boots stretched out before him, rocked by the soft swaying of the coach, and silent, as was his custom. All three rested their swords between their knees and were wearing their hats.

"There he is," said Guadalmedina.

Quevedo and Alatriste leaned toward the count to take a look. A black carriage similar to theirs, with no coat-of-arms on the door and with drawn curtains, had just passed the Torrecilla and was proceeding along the *paseo*. The coachman was dressed in brown, with one white and one green plume in his hat.

Guadalmedina opened the window behind the coach-box and gave instructions to the driver, who slapped the reins to catch up with the other carriage. They drove on for a short distance, until the first carriage stopped at a discreet nook beneath the branches of an old chestnut standing near a fountain topped with a stone dolphin. The second coach pulled up beside the first. Guadalmedina opened the door, and stepped down into the narrow space between them. Alatriste and Quevedo, removing their hats, did the same. And when the curtain of the black carriage was pulled back, they saw a strong, ruddy face hardened by dark, intelligent eyes; a ferocious beard and mustache; a large head set on powerful shoulders; and the crimson design of the cross of Calatrava. Those shoulders bore the weight of the largest monarchy on the earth, and they be-

longed to don Gaspar de Guzmán, Conde de Olivares, favorite of our lord and sovereign, Philip IV, King of All the
Spains.

"I did not expect to see you again so soon, Captain Alatriste," said Olivares. "You were on your way to Flanders."

"That was my intention, Excellency. But something
came up."

"So I see. Have you been told that you possess a rare
ability for complicating your life?"

It was an uncommon dialogue, especially given that it
was taking place between the favorite of the King of Spain
and an obscure swordsman. In the narrow space between
the two coaches, Guadalmedina and Quevedo listened in
silence. The Conde de Olivares had exchanged conventional
greetings with them, and was now addressing his remarks
to Captain Alatriste with a nearly courtly attention that
softened the hauteur of his severe countenance. Such deference from a favorite was not usual, a fact that escaped
no one.

"An astounding ability," Olivares repeated, as if to
himself.

The captain refrained from comment and waited quietly, hat doffed, with a respect not lacking aplomb. After a
last look at the captain, Olivares directed himself to Guadalmedina.

"About the issue that concerns us," he said, "you must

know that there is nothing to be done. I appreciate your information, but I can offer nothing in exchange. No one can intervene in the affairs of the Holy Office, not even our lord and king." He gestured with a broad, strong hand knotted with prominent veins. "Regardless, this is not something we can bother His Majesty with."

Álvaro de la Marca looked at Alatriste, whose expression had not changed, and then turned to Olivares. "No way out of it, then?"

"None. And I regret being unable to help you." There was a trace of condescending sincerity in the favorite's tone. "Especially because the shot aimed at our Captain Alatriste was also meant for me. But that is how things are."

Guadalmedina bowed. Despite his title of grandee of Spain he, too, was hatless before Olivares. Álvaro de la Marca was a courtier, and he knew that any give and take at court had its limits. For him, it was already a triumph that the most powerful man in the monarchy would grant him a minute of his time. Yet he persisted.

"Will the boy burn, Excellency?"

The favorite tugged at the Flemish lace falling from the wrists of his dark green-trimmed doublet, bare of jewels or adornment, austere, as decreed by the current edict against pomp and ostentation that he himself had urged the king to sign.

"I fear so," he said dispassionately. "And the girl. And

we can be thankful that there are no others to lead to the coals."

"How much time do we have left?"

"Very little. According to my information, they are speeding up the particulars of the trial, and it may be the Plaza Mayor within a couple of weeks. Considering the current state of my relationship with the Holy Office, that would be a feather in their caps." He shook his powerful head nested in the starched collar encircling a ruddy neck. "They have not forgiven me the business of the Genoese."

A slight, melancholy smile appeared between the dark beard on his chin and the fierce mustache, and he lifted his enormous hand to indicate the interview closed. Guadalmedina again bowed slightly, enough to be polite without compromising his honor.

"You have been very generous with your time. We are deeply grateful, and indebted to Your Lordship."

"You may expect a bill, don Álvaro. My Lordship never does anything gratis." The favorite turned toward don Francisco, who was playing the part of the stone guest in Tirso's *The Trickster of Seville*. "As for you, Señor de Quevedo, it is my hope that our relations may improve. A sonnet or two praising my policy in Flanders would not go unappreciated, one of those anonymous broadsheets that everyone knows are written by you. And a timely poem on the need to reduce by half the value of the *vellón* coin.

Something in the vein of those verses you had the kindness to devote to me the other day:

> *"May the courtly star that disposes you*
> *to the King's favor, without intent or vengeance,*
> *a miracle that curtails envy's diligence . . ."*

An uncomfortable don Francisco shot an oblique glance toward his companions. Following his long and painful exile from favor—which he had good signs of at last regaining—the poet hoped to recover his cachet at court, emerging from all his lawsuits and reversals of fortune. The events of the convent of Las Benitas came at an inopportune moment for him, and the fact that for an old debt of honor and friendship he would place his present good star in danger said a great deal for his character. Loathed and feared for his acerbic pen and his extraordinary wit, Quevedo had in recent days attempted not to appear hostile to the powers that be, and that had led him to intersperse his accustomed pessimistic vision and outbursts of bad humor with praise. Human after all, little inclined to return to exile, and hoping to shore up his waning estate, the great satirist was endeavoring to curb his pen, for fear of losing everything. Furthermore, he still sincerely believed, as many did, that Olivares could be the ironfisted surgeon needed to cure the aged and sickly Spanish lion.

It must be said, however, in defense of Alatriste's friend that, even during the times of his bonanza, Quevedo had written a play entitled *What Should the Favorite Be Like*, which did not argue well for the future Conde-Duque's influence at court. And despite the attempts of Olivares and other powers at court to attract the poet, that tenuous friendship burst apart some years later. Tittle-tattle had it that the king was irritated by a satiric poem he found beneath his napkin, although I think it was something of greater substance that turned them into mortal enemies, awakened the wrath of our lord and king, and was the cause of an old and ill Quevedo's being imprisoned in San Marcos de León.

That happened later, when the monarchy had become an insatiable machine for devouring taxes, while a drained populace received nothing in exchange but the political blunders and the disasters of war. Catalonia and Portugal rebelled, the French—as usual—wanted to slice off their share, and Spain plunged into civil war, ruin, and shame. But I will refer to such somber times at the proper moment. What I wish to relate now is that that evening in the Prado, the poet gave an austere but accommodating and nearly courtly reply.

"I shall consult the Muses, Excellency. And do what can be done."

Olivares nodded, already satisfied. "I have no doubt

you will." His tone was that of someone who does not re-
motely consider a different possibility. "As for your suit for
the eight thousand four hundred *reales* owed by the
Duque de Osuna, you know that things at the palace go
slowly. All in good time. Come by to see me some day and
we will have a leisurely chat. And do not forget my poem."

Quevedo nodded, not without a second slightly em-
barrassed glance toward his companions. He particularly
studied Guadalmedina, searching for a sign of mockery,
but Álvaro de la Marca was an experienced courtier; he
knew the sword-sharp gifts of the satirist, and his face
showed only the prudent expression of someone who has
heard nothing. The favorite turned to Diego Alatriste.

"As for you, Señor Captain, I regret that I cannot help
you." His tone, although again distant as befitted their rel-
ative positions, was amiable. "I confess that for some strange
reason, which perhaps both you and I recognize, I have a
certain fondness for your person. . . . That, in addition to
the request from my dear friend don Álvaro, caused me to
grant you this meeting. But you are aware that the more
power one obtains, the more limited is the opportunity to
exercise it."

Alatriste held his hat in one hand and rested the other
on the pommel of his sword. "With all respect, Your Excellency, one word from you can save that lad."

"I suppose that is true. In fact, an order signed by my

hand would be enough. But it is not that easy. That would place me in the position of having to make concessions in return. And in my office, concessions can be made only rarely. Your young friend weighs very little on the scales in relation to other serious burdens that God and our king have placed in my hands. So I have no choice but to wish you good fortune."

He concluded with an expression that boded no appeal; the matter was sealed. But Alatriste held his eyes without blinking.

"Excellency. I have nothing but the sword I live by and my record of service, which means nothing to anyone." The captain spoke very slowly, as if thinking aloud more than addressing the first minister of two worlds. "Neither am I a man of many words or resources. But they are going to burn an innocent lad whose father, my comrade, died fighting in those wars that are as much the king's as they are yours. Perhaps I, and Lope Balboa, and Balboa's son, do not tip the scale that Your Excellency so rightly mentioned. Yet one never knows what twists and turns life will take, nor whether one day the full reach of a good blade will not be more beneficial than all the papers and all the notaries and all the royal seals in the world. If you help the orphan of one of your soldiers, I give you my word that on such a day you can count on me."

Neither Quevedo nor Guadalmedina—no one—had

ever heard Diego Alatriste utter so many words at one time. And the king's favorite listened, inscrutable, motionless, with only an attentive gleam in his astute dark eyes. The captain had spoken with melancholy respect, but with a firmness that might have seemed brusque had it not been made amenable by his serene gaze and calm tone, totally devoid of arrogance. He seemed merely to have enunciated objective fact.

"I do not know whether it will be five, six, even ten days, months, or years hence," the captain persisted. "But you can count on me."

There was a long silence. Olivares, who had begun to close the coach door, concluding the interview, paused. Beneath his terrible mustache, Alatriste and his companions glimpsed something resembling a smile.

"'Sblood!" he said.

The favorite stared for what seemed an eternity. And then, very slowly, after removing a sheet of paper from a portfolio lined with Moroccan leather, he took a lead pencil and wrote four words: *Alquézar. Huesca. Green Book.* Pensively, he reread several times what he'd written. Finally, slowly, as if doubting what he was about to do until the last moment, he handed it to Diego Alatriste.

"You are absolutely right, Captain," he murmured, still thoughtful, before glancing toward the sword Alatriste wore on his left side. "In truth, one never knows."

VIII. A NOCTURNAL VISIT

The bells at San Jerónimo pealed twice as Diego Alatriste slowly turned the key. His initial apprehension turned to relief when the lock, oiled from inside that very evening, turned with a soft click.

He pushed the door, opening it in the darkness without the least squeak from its hinges. *Auro clausa patent.* With gold, doors open, Dómine Pérez would have said; and don Francisco de Quevedo had referred to don Dinero as a "powerful caballero." In truth, that the gold was from the pouch of the Conde de Guadalmedina and not from the thin purse of Captain Alatriste mattered not at all. No one cared about name, origin, or smell. The gold had bought the keys and the plan of the house, and thanks to it, some-one was going to receive a disagreeable surprise.

Alatriste had bid don Francisco good-bye a couple of

hours earlier, when he accompanied the poet to Calle de las Postas and watched him gallop away on a good horse, carrying traveling clothes, sword, portmanteau, a pistol in his saddletree, and, tucked in the band of his hat, those four words the Conde de Olivares had confided to them.

Guadalmedina, who had approved the poet's journey, had not shown the same enthusiasm for the adventure Alatriste was preparing to undertake that very night. Better to wait, he had said. But the captain could not wait. Quevedo's assignment was a shot in the dark. He had to do something in the meantime.

He unsheathed his dagger and, holding it in his left hand, crossed the patio, trying not to bump into anything in the dark and wake the servants. At least one of them—the one who had provided the keys and the plan to Álvaro de la Marca's agents—would sleep deaf, mute, and blind that night, but there were a half-dozen more who might take to heart his having disturbed their sleep at such hours. The captain had taken the appropriate precautions. He was wearing dark clothing, without a cape or hat to get in his way. In his belt was one of his flintlock pistols, well oiled and ready to fire, along with his sword and dagger. Finally he had added the old buffcoat that had offered such venerable service in a Madrid to which Alatriste himself had contributed, not a little, to making insalubrious. As for boots, they had been left in Juan Vicuña's little hideaway.

In their stead the captain was wearing a pair of leather sandals with woven grass soles, very useful for moving with the speed and silence of a shadow. The sandals were a lesson learned in times even more deadly than these, when a man had to slip between fascine battlements and trenches to slit the throats of Flemish heretics during cruel night raids in which no quarter was given or expected.

The house was still and dark. Alatriste bumped against the rim of a cistern, felt his way around it, and finally found the door he was seeking. The second key worked to his satisfaction, and the captain found himself in a broad, enclosed stairway. He went up the stairs, holding his breath, grateful that the steps were stone and not creaking wood. At the top, he paused in the shelter of a large armoire to orient himself. Then he took a few paces forward, hesitated in the shadowy corridor, counted two doors to the right, and went in, *vizcaína* in hand, holding his sword to prevent it from knocking against some piece of furniture. Next to the window, Luis de Alquézar was snoring like a pig, in deep shadow relieved by the soft glow of an oil lamp. Diego Alatriste could not contain a secret smile: his powerful enemy, the royal secretary, was afraid of the dark.

Alquézar, only half awake, was slow to understand that he was not having a nightmare. But when he started to turn

onto his other side and the sharp gouge of a dagger beneath his chin prevented him, he realized this was not a
bad dream. Frightened, he tried to sit up, blinked his eyes,
and opened his mouth to scream, but Diego Alatriste's
hand quickly covered it.

"One word," whispered the captain, "and you are a
dead man."

Between the nightcap and the iron hand that was gag-
ging him, the eyes and mustache of the royal secretary
were quivering with terror. A few inches from his face, the
weak light of the lamp outlined Alatriste's aquiline profile, the luxuriant mustache, the sharp blade of the dagger.

"Do you have armed guards?" asked the captain.

Alquézar shook his head no. His breath moistened the
palm of the captain's hand.

"Do you know who I am?"

The terrified eyes blinked, and after an instant the head
nodded affirmatively. And when Alatriste took his hand
away from Luis de Alquézar's mouth, he did not try to shout.
Mouth agape, frozen with stupor, he stared at the shadow
bending over him as if seeing a ghost. The captain pressed
the tip of the dagger a little harder against Alquézar's throat.

"What are you going to do with the boy?" demanded
Alatriste.

Alquézar's bulging eyes saw nothing but the dagger.

His nightcap had fallen onto the pillow, and the lamp illuminated sparse, tangled, greasy hair that accentuated his
ignoble round face, heavy nose, and short, scraggly beard.

"I do not know whom you mean."

The royal secretary's voice was weak and hoarse, but
even the threat of the steel could not mask his indignation. Alatriste pressed the dagger until he evoked a moan.

"Then I will kill you right now, sure as there is a God."

Alquézar moaned again. He was petrified, not daring
to blink. The sheets and his nightshirt stank of bitter
sweat, fear, and hatred.

"It is not in my hands," he babbled finally. "The Inquisition . . ."

"Don't fuck with me. Not the Inquisition. Fray Emilio
Bocanegra and you, just you two."

Very slowly Alquézar lifted a conciliatory hand, never
taking his eyes from the dagger pressing against his
throat. "Perhaps something . . ." he murmured. "We could
perhaps try . . ."

He was frightened, but it was also true that in the light
of day, when that dagger was not at his throat, the royal
secretary's attitude could change. No doubt it would, but
Alatriste had nothing to lose by trying.

"If anything happens to the boy," he said, his face only
inches away from Alquézar's, "I will come back here as I

have come tonight. I will come to kill you like a dog, slit your throat while you sleep."

"I tell you again that the Inquisition . . ."

The oil in the lamp sputtered, and for a moment its light reflected in the captain's eyes was a spark from the flames of Hell. "While you sleep," he repeated, and beneath the hand resting on Alquézar's chest, he could feel that the man was shaking. "I swear it."

No one would have doubted this for an instant, and the royal secretary's gaze reflected that certainty. But the captain also saw his relief at knowing he was not going to be killed that night. In the world of this loathsome creature, night was night and day was day, and like a new chess game, everything could begin again in the morning. And suddenly, like a revelation, Alatriste realized that the royal secretary would be back in command the moment the dagger was removed. The knowledge that despite anything he could do, I was already sentenced to death, filled Alatriste with an icy, hopeless rage. He hesitated, and Alquézar immediately perceived that hesitation with alarm. In one terrible flash, as if the steel of the *vizcaína* transmitted a glimpse of Alquézar's sinister thoughts, the captain saw everything clearly.

"If you kill me now," Alquézar said slowly, "nothing will save the boy."

It was true. But neither would the boy be saved if he

left this man alive. With that, the captain stepped back a little, just enough to allow a brief reflection upon whether it was a good idea to slit the royal secretary's throat here and now, and at least leave one fewer serpent in that nest of vipers. But my fate stayed his arm. He turned to take a look around him, as if needing space for his thoughts, and as he turned, his elbow struck a water jug on the night table, something he had not seen in the darkness. The jug exploded on the floor with a sound like a harquebus shot. Alatriste, still indecisive, bent to put his dagger back to his enemy's throat, just as a light appeared in the doorway. The captain looked up to see Angélica de Alquézar in her nightdress, a candle in her hand, surprised and sleepy-eyed, taking in the scene.

From that instant on, everything happened in rapid succession. The girl screamed, a piercing, bloodcurdling scream that was not fear but malice. It was long and drawn out, like the cry of a female falcon when a predator steals her chicks. It rang through the night, raising every hair on Alatriste's head. Befuddled, he tried to move away from the bed, with the dagger still in his hand and not knowing what the devil to do with the girl; Angélica was already across the room, fleet as a shot.

Dropping the candle to the floor, she threw herself on

the captain like a tiny Fury, all blond curls and white silk nightdress floating in the darkness like the shroud of a ghost—beautiful, he supposed, although feminine charms were the last thing on his mind. She fastened onto the arm with the dagger and bit into him like a small blond bull-dog. And there she hung, teeth clamped onto his arm, tenaciously clinging to the frightened Alatriste, who in his attempt to shake her off lifted her right off the floor. But she did not budge. Occupied with her, the captain watched the girl's uncle, liberated from the *vizcaína* that had been threatening him, leap from the bed with unexpected vigor, and rush, barelegged and in his nightshirt, to an armoire where he seized a short sword, yelling, "Murderers! Intruders! To arms!" and other such cries. Upon which Alatriste heard the house stirring: thudding footsteps and voices torn from sleep—in all, the tumult of a thousand demons.

Finally the captain succeeded in shaking the girl loose, with a cuff from his free hand that sent her rolling across the floor. Just in time he dodged a thrust from Luis de Alquézar, who, had he not been so undone by his fright, would then and there have put an end to Alatriste's adventurous career. The harried intruder, continuing to avoid Alquézar's blade in a chase that encompassed the entire room, put that same hand to his sword, turned, and drove Alquézar back with a two-handed swing. He then headed toward the door to make his escape, but again ran into the girl, who renewed her assault with a bellicose screech that would have turned an ordinary man's blood to ice in his veins.

Again Angélica charged, ignoring the sword Alatriste held uselessly in front of him, and which he had to raise at the last instant to keep from skewering the girl like a chicken on a spit. In the blink of an eye, the angelic-looking Angélica again clamped tooth and nail into his arm as he danced from one corner of the room to the other, unable to rid himself of her, so encumbered that he could do nothing but parry the sword that Alquézar, without a thought for his niece, was swinging with murderous intent. This chase might have lasted through eternity, but Alatriste somehow pushed the girl aside and made a thrust at Alquézar that drove the royal secretary staggering back amid a great clatter of basins, urinals, and assorted pottery.

At last the captain was in the corridor, but only in time to spy three or four servants running up the steps brandishing their weapons. It was a bad scenario. So bad that he pulled out his pistol and fired point-blank at the men on the stairway, a confused tangle of legs, arms, swords, bucklers, and clubs. Before they had time to regroup, he ran back into the room, shot the bolt of the door, and sped like an exhalation toward the window, but not before dodging two thrusts of Alquézar's sword and, for the third, unholy time, finding the girl clinging like a leech to his arm, biting and clawing with a ferocity unsuspected in a girl of twelve. Somehow the captain reached the window, kicked open the shutter, and slit the nightshirt of Alquézar, who was staggering clumsily toward the bed, covering himself. As Alatriste threw one leg over the iron balcony he was still shaking his arm and trying to loose Angélica's hold. The blue eyes and tiny white teeth, which don Luis de Góngora—begging Señor de Quevedo's pardon—had described as *aljófares*, minute pearls set between lips like rose petals, were flashing with exceptional ferocity, until Alatriste, now fed to *his* teeth with the whole matter, grabbed her by her curly locks and pulled her off his mar-tyred arm, tossing her through the air like a furious, scream-ing rag doll. She landed upon her uncle and both of them crashed onto the bed, which spread its legs and collapsed noisily to the floor.

At that point, the captain dropped from the window, ran across the patio and out to the street. He did not stop running until he had left that nightmare far behind.

Alatriste stayed in the shelter of the shadows, seeking the darkest streets by which to return to Juan Vicuña's gaming house. He went down Cava Alta and Cava Baja, along

Posada de la Villa and past the shuttered shop of the apothecary Fadrique, before crossing Puerta Cerrada, where at that early hour not a soul was stirring.

He did not want to think, but it was inevitable that he would. He was certain of having committed a stupid act that only made a bad situation worse. A cold rage pounded in his pulse and blood hammered at his temples, and he would gladly have beat himself in the face to give vent to his desperation and his anger. It was the impulse to do something, not to keep waiting for others to act for him—he told himself once he had recovered a little calm—that had brought him out of his den like a desperate wolf, on the hunt for he knew not what.

It was not like him. Life, however long it lasted, was much simpler when there was no one to look out for but oneself. It was a difficult world in which every day a throat was slit, and nobody had any responsibility but to keep one's own skin and life intact. Diego Alatriste y Tenorio, veteran of the *tercios* of Flanders and galleys of Naples, had spent long years ridding himself of any sentiment he could not resolve with a sword. But now look where he was. A boy whose name he had not even known a short while ago was turning everything upside down, making him aware that every man, however able-bodied he may be, has chinks in his armor.

And speaking of chinks. Alatriste felt his left forearm, still aching from Angélica's bites, and could not prevent a grimace of admiration. At times, tragedies have all the earmarks of burlesque, he told himself. That tiny blond cat, of whom he had heard only vague references—though I myself had never mentioned her name, and the captain knew nothing of my relationship with her—had showed uncommon promise of ferociousness, displaying bloodlines worthy of her uncle.

Finally, remembering once again Luis de Alquézar's terrified eyes, the moist breath on the hand that had silenced him, his stench of sweat and fear, Alatriste shrugged. At last his soldier's stoicism was taking hold. *After all,* he concluded, *we can never foresee the consequences of our acts.* At the least, following the nocturnal surprise he had just experienced, Luis de Alquézar now knew he was vulnerable. His neck was just as much at the mercy of a dagger as anyone else's, and having seen that clearly could be as bad ultimately as it was good.

With that, the captain at last reached the small Conde de Barajas plaza, a step or two from the Plaza Mayor, and as he was about to turn the corner he saw light and a number of people. It was definitely not the hour of the *paseo,* so he hid in a doorway. Perhaps it was some of Juan Vicuña's clients leaving after a nightlong skirmish with the cards, or early-morning adventurers . . . or the Law. Whoever it was, this was no time to meet anyone unexpectedly and risk a confrontation.

By the light of a lantern they had set on the ground, he watched as men pasted up a handbill near the Cuchilleros arch, and then moved down the street. There were five of them, armed, and they carried a roll of broadsheets and a bucket of paste. Alatriste would have gone along without paying any attention to what they were doing, had he not noticed that one of them was carrying the black baton of the Inquisition's *familiares*. As soon as they were out of sight, he went to the poster and tried to read it, but there was no light. The paste was fresh, however, and he tore the paper from the wall, folded it twice, and took it with him up the steps beneath the arch. He went straight to the pillars in the plaza, opened Juan Vicuña's secret door, and once in the passageway struck a spark with flint, lit tinder, and then a candle stub. He did all this while forcing himself to be patient, the way one dawdles before breaking the seals on a letter that might bear bad news. And bad news there was. The poster was an announcement from the Holy Office.

Be it known to all citizens and dwellers of this Town, and the Court of His Majesty, that the Holy Office of the Inquisition will celebrate a public Auto-da-Fé in the Plaza Mayor of this City on Sunday next, the fourth day ...

In spite of the grim way that Captain Alatriste earned a living, he was not a man who often took God's name in vain, but this time he let loose with a blasphemous soldier's oath that made the candle flame tremble. It was less than a week till the fourth day of the new month, and there was not a blessed thing he could do until then except wait, damning all his Devils. Add to that the possibility that following his nocturnal visit to the royal secretary, they would on the morning paste up another broadside, this time from the *corregidor*, announcing a price for his head. He wadded up the paper and stood leaning against the wall, staring into empty space.

He had burned all his powder with the exception of one last shot. Now his only hope was don Francisco de Quevedo.

Your Mercies must forgive me if I again turn to my own story, there in the dungeon of the secret prisons of Toledo, where I had lost nearly any notion of time, or of day and night. After several more sessions, with corresponding beatings by the redheaded guard—they say that Judas had red hair, and my torturer fulfilled his days as Christ's betrayer concluded his—and without having revealed anything worthy of mention, they left me more or less in peace. Elvira de la Cruz's accusation, and Angélica's amulet, seemed to be all they needed, and the last truly difficult session had consisted of a tedious interrogation based on many "That is not true," "Tell the truth," and "Confess that," in which they repeatedly asked me the names of my supposed accomplices, thrashing me with that pizzle in response to every silence, which was every time. I shall say only that I stood firm and did not speak any name. I was so weak that the fainting I had at first feigned, and that had had such conclusive results, now happened naturally, saving me from a true Calvary. I'll wager that if my torturers did not go further it was out of fear of depriving themselves of the starring role they were preparing for me during the festival in the Plaza Mayor.

I did not examine these details too closely, though, for I was far from lucid, so addled that I did not recognize myself in the Íñigo who took the beatings or who waked with a shudder in the darkness of a dank cell, listening to a rat scamper back and forth across the floor. My one true anxiety was that I would rot in that cell until I was fourteen, at which time I would make close acquaintance of the rope and wood contrivance still standing in the interrogation room, as if signaling that sooner or later I would be its prey.

In the meantime, I chased the rat. I was tired of going to sleep dreading its bites, and I devoted many hours to studying the situation. I ended up knowing its habits better than my own: its chariness—it was an old veteran rat—its audacity, the way it moved inside the walls. I learned to follow its scamperings, even in the dark. One night, pretending to be asleep, I let it follow its usual routine until I knew it was in the corner where I had set out bread crumbs every day, enticing it to that spot. I grabbed the water jug and slammed it down, with such good fortune that it turned up its paws and died, without squeaking an "Ay!" or whatever the devil rats say when they get what is coming to them.

That night, finally, I could sleep peacefully. But the next morning I began to miss my cellmate. Its absence left me time to reflect on other things, such as Angélica's treachery and the stake where I could, and almost certainly would, end my brief life.

As for their burning me to a crisp, I can say, without braggadocio, that I spent no time at all worrying about that. I was so exhausted by the prison and the torture that any change would seem like a liberation. I often busied myself in calculating how long it would take to burn to death. Then again, if one recants in the proper form, they will use the garrote before lighting the pyre, and the end will come more gently. Whatever they did, I consoled myself, no suffering is eternal; and ultimately there is peace. Furthermore, in those days dying was a common occurrence, easily accomplished. I had not committed sins enough to weigh down my soul to the point of preventing my rejoining, in whatever place, that good soldier Lope Balboa. At my age, and having a certain heroic concept of life—do not forget that I was in these straits because I had not informed on the captain or his friends—the situation was made bearable by considering it a test in which, again begging your pardon, I found I was quite pleased with my performance. I do not know if in truth I truly was a lad with natural courage; but the Lord God above knows that if the first step toward courage consists of comporting oneself as if one were indeed courageous, I—let the record show—had taken not a few of those steps.

Nevertheless, I was hopelessly melancholy, filled with a deep anguish—something akin to wanting to cry but which had nothing to do with the tears of pain or physical weakness that were sometimes spilled. It was instead a cold, sorrowful sadness related to the memory of my mother and my little sisters, the captain's look when he silently approved of something I had done, the soft green hillsides around Oñate, my childhood games with boys who had lived nearby. I regretted that I had to bid farewell to all that forever, and I mourned all the beautiful things that had awaited me in life, and that now I would never have. And especially, more than anything, I was sad not

to look for one last time into the eyes of Angélica de
Alquézar.

I swear to Your Mercies that I could not hate her. Just the
opposite, knowing that she had played a part in my misfortune left a bittersweet taste that heightened the sorcery
of her memory. She was wicked—and she became more so
with time, I swear in Christ's name—but she was breath-
takingly beautiful. And it was precisely the combination
of evil and beauty, so tightly entwined, that fascinated me,
an agonizing pleasure as I suffered every torment because
of her. By my faith, one would think I was enchanted.
Later, as the years went by, I heard stories of men whose
souls had been stolen by a wily Devil, and in each of them
I recognized my own rapture. Angélica de Alquézar held
my soul in thrall, and she kept it as long as she lived.

And I, who would have killed for her a thousand times,
and died for her another thousand without blinking an
eye, will never forget her incomparable smile, her cold blue
eyes, her snowy white skin, so soft and smooth, the touch
still on my own skin, now covered with ancient scars, some
of which, *pardiez*, she herself gave me. Like the one on my
back, a long scar from a dagger, as indelible as that night,
long after the time I am writing about here, when we were
no longer children, and I held her in my arms, both loving
and hating her, not caring whether I would be dead or

alive at dawn. When she, so close to me, whispering through lips red from kissing my wound, spoke the words I shall never forget, in this life or in the next: *"I am happy I have not killed you yet."*

Frightened, prudent, or perhaps astute, if not all of those things, Luis de Alquézar was a patient crow, and he had the cards to play the game by his rules. So he was careful not to give the advantage to anyone. Diego Alatriste's name was not broadcast anywhere, and he spent the day, like all the previous ones, out of sight in the room in Juan Vicuña's gaming house. But during that period, the captain's nights were more active than his days, and in the dark of the next one, he made another visit to an old acquaintance.

The chief constable, Martín Saldaña, found him at the doorway of his house on Calle León when he returned from his last rounds. Or, to be more exact, what he encountered was the light glancing off Alatriste's pistol, which was aimed straight at him. But Saldaña was an even-tempered man who had, in the course of his life, seen more than his share of pistols, harquebuses, and every other kind of weapon pointed at him. This one made him neither hotter nor colder than usual. He propped his fists on his hips and stared at Diego Alatriste who, in cape and hat, was holding his pistol in his right hand and, to be safe, resting the left on the handle of the dagger stowed in his belt above his left kidney.

"'Pon 'is body, Diego, you like to tempt fate."

Alatriste did not respond. He stepped a little out of the shadow to search Saldaña's face by the faint light from the street—just a large candle burning at the corner of Calle de las Huertas. Then the captain turned up the barrel of the pistol, as if intending to show the weapon to his friend.

"Do I need this?"

Saldaña observed him an instant. "No," he said finally. "Not this minute."

That broke the tension. The captain stuffed the pistol back into his belt and dropped his hand from the dagger.

"We are going to take a little walk," he said.

"What I cannot understand," said Alatriste, "is why they are not openly looking for me."

They were walking across Antón Martín plaza toward Calle Atocha, deserted at that hour. There was still a waning moon in the sky, which had just emerged from behind the chapel of the Amor de Dios Hospital, and its beams rippled on the water falling from the curbstone of a fountain and running in rivulets down the street. There was a smell of rotted vegetables in the air, and the pungent odor of mule and horse manure.

"I don't know, and I do not want to know," said Saldaña. "But it is true that no one has given your name to the authorities."

He stepped to one side to avoid some mud, but put his foot where he least wanted and choked back a curse behind his graying beard. His short cape accentuated his stocky build and broad shoulders.

"Whatever the case," he continued, "be very careful. The fact that my catchpoles are not on your trail does not mean that no one is interested in the state of your health. According to my information, the *familiares* of the Inquisition have orders to bring you in with maximum discretion."

"Have they told you why?"

Saldaña threw a sideways glance toward the captain. "I haven't been told, and I do not want to know. One fact: they have identified the woman who was found dead the other day in the sedan chair. She is one María Montuenga. She served as a duenna to a novice in the convent of La Adoración Benita. Do you know the name?"

"Never heard it."

"So I imagined." The chief constable laughed quietly to himself. "Better that way, because whatever else is going on, this is a rather murky business. They say that the old woman was a procuress, and now the Inquisition is involved. . . . That would not ring a bell either, I imagine."

"None."

"Right. They are also talking about some bodies that no one has seen, and about a certain convent turned upside down in the midst of a hurly-burly that no one seems to remember." Again that sideways glance at Alatriste. "There are those who connect all this with Sunday's *auto-da-fé*."

"And you?"

"I make no connections. I receive orders and I carry them out. And when no one tells me anything, a circumstance I greatly celebrate in this case, all I do is watch, listen, and keep my mouth shut. Which is not a bad position to take in my office. As for you, Diego, I would like to see you far away from all this. Why are you still in town?"

"I can't leave. Íñigo . . ."

Saldaña interrupted him with a strong oath.

"I don't want to hear it. I have already told you that I do not want to know anything concerning your Íñigo, or anything else. As for Sunday, I do have something to say about that. Stay away. I have orders to place all my constables, armed to the teeth, at the disposition of the Holy Office. Whatever happens, neither you nor the Blessed Mother of God will be able to move a finger."

The swift black shadow of a cat crossed their path. They were near the tower of the Hospital de la Concepción, and a woman's voice cried out, "Watch out below!" Wisely, they jumped aside, and heard the chamber pot being emptied onto the street from above.

"One last thing," said Saldaña. "There is a certain swordsman you must keep an eye out for. Apparently, parallel to the official plot, there is a semi-official one."

"What plot are you referring to?" And in the darkness, Alatriste smirked and twisted his mustache. "I thought I just heard you say that you know nothing at all."

"The Devil take you, Captain."

"They want me to wake with the Devil, that is true."

"Well, blast it, do not let that happen." Saldaña adjusted his cape more comfortably around his shoulders, and his pistols and all the iron he wore at his waist clinked lugubriously. "That person I was speaking of is going around making inquiries about you. He has recruited half a dozen of those big talkers to fillet your innards before you have time to say 'good day.' The bastard's name is . . ."

"Malatesta. Gualterio Malatesta."

Martín Saldaña's quiet laugh was heard again. "The very one," he confirmed. "Italian, I believe."

"From Sicily. Once we worked together. Or rather, we did half a job together. We have crossed paths another time or two since then."

"Well, by Christ, you did not leave a pleasant memory behind. I believe he very much wants to see you."

"What more do you know of him?"

"Very little. He has the support of powerful sponsors, and he is good at his trade. Apparently he went around Genoa and Naples, killing right and left on behalf of others. They say he enjoys it. He lived a time in Seville, and he has been here in Madrid about a year. If you want, I can make further inquiries."

Alatriste did not answer. They had come to the far end of El Prado de Atocha, and before them lay the empty darkness of the gardens, the meadow, and the start of the road to Vallecas. They stood quietly, listening to the chirping of crickets. It was Saldaña who spoke first.

"Use caution on Sunday," he said in a low voice, as if the place were filled with indiscreet listeners. "I would not like to have to put you in shackles. Or kill you."

Still the captain said nothing. Wrapped in his cape, he had not moved. Beneath the brim of his hat, his face was darker than the night.

Saldaña breathed a hoarse sigh, took a few steps as if to leave, sighed again, and stopped with an ill-humored "I swear by all that's holy."

"Listen, Diego," Saldaña continued. Like Alatriste, he was staring into the dark meadow. "Neither you nor I have many illusions about the world it has been our lot to live in. I am weary. I have a beautiful wife and employ that I like and that allows me to save a little. That makes it necessary, when I am carrying my lieutenant's staff, for me not to know my own father. I may in fact be a whoreson, but I am *my own* whoreson. I would like for you——"

"You talk too much, Martín."

The captain had spoken softly, in an abstracted tone. Saldaña removed his hat and ran one of his broad hands across a skull barely covered with hair.

"You're right. I talk too much. Maybe because I am getting old." He sighed for the third time, eyes still focused on the darkness, listening to the crickets. "We are both getting old, Captain. You and I."

In the distance, they heard bells marking the hour. Alatriste did not move. "We haven't many years left," the captain said.

"Not many at all, *pardiez.*" The chief constable put on his hat, hesitated an instant, and then walked back to the captain, stopping at his side. "There are not many who share our memories and silences. And of them, few are the men they used to be."

He whistled an old military tune. A little song about the old *tercios,* raids, plunder, and victories. They had sung it together, with my father and other comrades, eighteen years before in the sacking of Ostend and on the long march from the Rhine toward Friesland with don Ambrosio Spínola, when they took Oldenzaal and Lingen.

"But it may be true," Saldaña said in conclusion, "that

this century no longer deserves men like us. I am referring to the men we once were."

Once again he looked toward Alatriste. The captain slowly nodded.

The thin moon cast a vague, formless shadow at their feet.

"It may be," the captain murmured, "that we do not deserve them either."

IX. *AUTO-DA-FÉ*

The Spain of the fourth Philip, like that of his predecessors, was enchanted with the ritual burning of heretics and Jews. An *auto-da-fé* attracted thousands of spectators, from aristocracy to the lowest townsman. And when one was celebrated in Madrid, it was witnessed from the loges of honor by Their Majesties the king and queen. Even Queen Isabel, who, because she was young, and French, was at first repelled by such activities, eventually became an enthusiast, like everyone else. The only thing Spanish the daughter of Henri the Béarnaise never accepted was to live in El Escorial, which she always found too cold, too grand, and too sinister for her taste. She was, however, subjected to that vexation posthumously: having never wanted to set foot inside it, she was buried there after her death. Though it is not such a bad place to be, God knows, laid to rest alongside the imposing tombs of Emperor Charles the Fifth and his son the great Philip, ancestors of our fourth Austrian monarchy. Thanks to whom—great leaders that they were, whether for bad or ill, and to the despair of Turks, French, Dutch, English, and the whore who birthed them all—Spain, for a century and a half, had Europe and the world by their tender testicles.

But let us return to the bonfire. Preparations for the fiesta, in which, to my misfortune, I had a reserved place, began a day or two before the event. There was great activity by carpenters and other workmen in the Plaza Mayor, where they were constructing a high platform fifty feet long facing an amphitheater of stair-stepped benches, draperies, tapestries, and damasks. Not even for the wedding of Their Majesties had such industry and facilities been on display. All the streets into the plaza were blocked so that coaches and horses would not clog free movement, and for the royal family, a canopy had been rigged on Los Mercaderes, as that location offered the most shade. Since the *auto* was a long ceremony, taking the whole day, there were stands, protected from the sun by a canvas, where one could get a cool drink and something to eat. It was decided that for the convenience of the august persons of the king and queen, they would enter their loge from the palace of the Conde de Barajas, using an elevated passageway over

Cava San Miguel that communicated with the count's houses on the plaza.

Expectations resulting from this level of preparation were so high that vying for tickets to a seat at a balconied window often deteriorated into a battle royal. Many people of influence paid good ducats to the Lord Chamberlain of His Majesty's household to obtain the best locations, including ambassadors, grandees, the king's courtiers, council presidents, and even His Holiness the Papal Nuncio, who never missed a bullfight, a tournament of tilting, or an outdoor roasting, not even for a *fumata blanca* in Rome.

On a day like this, meant to be memorable, the Holy Office wanted to kill several partridges with a single shot. Resolved to undermine the Conde de Olivares's policy of rapprochement with the Jewish Portuguese bankers, the most radical inquisitors of the Supreme Council had planned a spectacular *auto-da-fé* that would strike fear into the heart of any who were not secure in the purity of their blood. The message was clear. However much of Olivares's money and favor they might have, Portuguese of Hebrew blood would never be safe in Spain. The Inquisition, relentlessly appealing to the religious conscience of our lord and king—as irresolute and easily influenced as a young man as he was when old, pleasant by nature but lacking character—preferred a ruined nation to one whose faith was threatened. And that preference, which in the long run had its effect—predictably, a most disastrous effect—upon Olivares's economic plans, was the principal reason why the trial was being hastened: to serve as an efficacious example to the public. What ordinarily would take months, even years, of assiduous instruction was completed in a few weeks' time.

Because of the haste, details of complex protocol were greatly simplified. Sentences were usually read to the penitents the night prior to the dreaded day, following a solemn procession of officials carrying the green cross destined for the plaza and the white one that would be raised above the stake. This time they were left to be made public on the day of the *auto-da-fé*, when everyone was already present for the festivities. Prisoners destined for the *auto* had arrived from the dungeons of Toledo the day before. They—we—were about twenty, and were housed in cells the Holy Office maintained on Calle de los Premostenses, darkly referred to as Calle de la Inquisición, very near the Santo Domingo plaza.

I was brought there on a Saturday night, having communicated with no one since I was taken from my cell and placed in a coach with closed curtains and a heavy guard. I never left the coach until I descended by torchlight in Madrid among the armed civilian *familiares* of the Inquisition. They led me down to a cell, where I was given a tol-

erable dinner, a blanket, and a straw mattress. I anticipated
a restless night as I listened to footsteps and the noise of
locks and bolts outside my door, voices coming and going,
a lot of scurrying about, and objects being rolled and
dragged. With which I began to fear that I could look forward to a very difficult day on the morrow.

I racked my brain, searching through dangerous moments I had witnessed in the playhouses of the *comedias,*
hoping that, as always happened there, I would find a way
out. At that point, I was certain that whatever my crime, I
would not be burned because of my age. But the prospect
of beatings and imprisonment, perhaps for life, were
strong possibilities, and I was not certain which seemed
worse. Nevertheless, the resilience of youth, the terrible
times I had survived, and the exhaustion of the journey,
soon took their natural course, and after a period of wake-
fulness in which I asked myself over and over how I had
come to that sad fate, I sank into a merciful and restorative
sleep that eased the restlessness of thought.

Two thousand people had stayed up all night to be assured
of a place in the Plaza Mayor, and by seven in the morning there was no room for another soul. Blending in
among the multitude, with the brim of his hat over his
face and a short cape thrown over his shoulders and across

the lower part of his face, Diego Alatriste made his way toward the de la Carne section of the plaza. The arches were jammed with people of every state and condition: hidalgos, clergy, artisans, servant girls, merchants, lackeys, students, rogues, beggars, and assorted rabble pushed and shoved in their quest for a good view. The balconied windows of the surrounding buildings were black with people of quality: gold chains, silver trimmings, fine cottons, one-hundred-*escudo* laces, nuns' habits, and men clad in the uniforms of chivalric orders, some bedecked with the insignia of the Golden Fleece. And below in the street, whole families assembled, including children, carrying baskets of victuals and drinks for luncheon and tea. Mead vendors, water sellers, and peddlers of sweets made hay while the sun shone down. A merchant with religious prints and rosaries hawked his merchandise at the top of his lungs; on a day such as this, he argued, these articles carried the blessing of the pope and plenary indulgences. A few feet away, a man who claimed to have been mutilated in Flanders, but who had never glimpsed a pike in his life, was plaintively begging, and squabbling over his place with a malingering cripple and another man hoarsely whining about scald head, a condition visible in the scales on his hairless head. Elegant young bloods were punning and playing with words, and whores were cajoling and wheedling. One woman, pretty but not wearing a mantle, and another who was, but whose mud-ugly face showed evidence of mercury poisoning—the kind who swore not to stroll down the garden path until they captured a grandee of Spain or a Genoese banker—were pleading with a common artisan, who had been flashing his sword and putting on airs, to loosen his purse strings and treat them to a tray of fruit or some candied almonds. And the poor man, who in all the excitement, had already let go of the two pieces of eight he had on him, congratulated himself for not bringing more—unaware, foolish man he was, that true señores never pay, or even pretend to; instead they make a show of *not* paying.

It was a luminous day, perfect for the momentous events to come, and the captain, his gray-green eyes dazzled by the blue spilling down the eaves onto the plaza, squinted against the sun as he elbowed his way through the crowd. It smelled of sweat, of too many people, of fiesta. He felt a hopeless desperation building inside him, impotence at confronting something that exceeded his limited forces. That machinery of the Inquisition was moving inexorably forward, leaving no opening for anything other than resignation and fear. He could do nothing; he himself was not safe there. He roamed among the crowd with his mustache pointed over his shoulder, retreating the minute someone looked at him a little longer than was wont. In truth, he kept moving just to be doing something, not to be glued to one of the columns in the arches. He asked himself where the devil don Francisco de Quevedo might be at this hour. His journey, whatever the result, was now the one thread of hope before the inevitable.

It was a thread he felt snap when he heard the trumpets of the guard, making him turn and look toward the crimson canopy-covered balcony on the façade of Los Mercaderes. Our lord and king, the queen, and the court were taking their seats amid the applause of the throng. Our fourth Philip, grave, impassive as a statue, made not a flicker of movement, not a foot, not a hand, not his head, as blond as the gold passementerie and the chain across his chest. Our queen wore yellow satin and a headdress of plumes and jewels. Guards with halberds took up posts beneath Their Majesties' balcony, Spanish on one side and German on the other, archers in the center, all of them impressive in their rigid order.

It was a handsome spectacle for anyone not in danger of being burned alive. The green cross was installed above the platform, and on the fronts of the buildings were hung, in alternating sequence, the coat-of-arms of His Majesty and that of the Inquisition: a cross between a sword and an olive branch. Everything was rigorously canonical. The spectacle could begin.

.   .   .

They had brought us from our cells at six-thirty in the morning, between constables and the *familiares* of the Holy Office armed with swords, pikes, and harquebuses. We were led in a procession through the Santo Domingo plaza, down San Ginés, and from there, crossing Calle Mayor, into the plaza by way of Calle de los Boteros. Marching in file, we were escorted by armed guards and mourning-clad *familiares* carrying sinister black staffs. There were clerics in surplices, dirges, lugubrious drums, cloth-covered crosses, and masses of people in the streets. And in the center of it all, here we came. First, the blasphemers, then the bigamous; after them, the sodomites and the Judaizers and the followers of Mohammed; and last, the practitioners of witchcraft. Each group included wax, cardboard, and rag representations of those who had died in prison and those who were fugitives, to be burned in effigy.

I was near the middle of the procession, among the minor Judaizers, so dazed that I thought I was in a dream from which, with a little effort and great relief, I would awake at any moment. We were all wearing sanbenitos, long white garments the guards had dressed us in as they took us from our cells. Mine bore a red St. Andrew's cross, but the others were painted with the flames of Hell. There were men, women, even a girl about my age. Some were weeping, and others were stone-faced, like the young priest who had denied at mass that God was in the host, the *forma sagrada,* and who refused to retract what he had said. One woman denounced as a witch by her neighbors, too old to stand on her own, and a man whose legs had been crippled during his torture, were riding mules. The most serious offenders were wearing cone hats, and all of us were carrying candles. Elvira de la Cruz was clad in sanbenito and cone hat, and when we were lined up, she was among the last. After we began to walk, I could no longer see her. I went with my head bowed, afraid I would see someone I knew among the people watching us pass by. As Your Mercies may imagine, I was mortified with shame.

As the procession filed into the plaza, the captain searched for me among the penitents. He could not find me until they made us climb up onto the platform and take a seat on the graduated steps, each of us between two *familiares.* Even then he had difficulty, for as I have told you I tried to keep my head down; in addition, the platform was easily seen from the windows, but the view of people standing in the arches was obstructed. The sentences had not yet been read publicly, so Alatriste was tremendously relieved when he saw that I was among the group of minor Judaizers, and not wearing the cone hat. That at least eliminated the stake as my possible fate.

Dominicans in their black-and-white habits could be seen moving among the black-clad constables of the Inquisition, organizing everything. The representatives of other orders—all except the Franciscans, who had refused to attend because they considered it a grave insult to be assigned a place behind the Augustinians—were already in their seats in places of honor, along with the Lord Chamberlain of His Majesty's household and councilors from Castile, Aragon, Italy, Portugal, Flanders, and the Indies. Beside the Inquisitor General, in the area reserved for the Tribunal of Six Judges, was Fray Emilio Bocanegra, bony and malevolent. He was savoring his day of triumph, as Luis de Alquézar must have been, seated in the loge of the highest palace officials, close to the balcony where at that moment our lord and king was swearing to defend the Catholic Church and to persecute heretics and apostates who opposed the true Faith.

The Conde de Olivares occupied a more discreet window to the right of their august majesties, and was looking very grim. It escaped very few who knew the secrets at court that this entire performance was in his honor.

The reading of the sentences began. One by one, penitents were led before the tribunal and there, after a detailed recitation of their crimes and sins, their fate was announced. Those who were to be lashed, or who were being sent to the galleys, moved on, roped together; then those destined for the stake followed, hands bound. Those latter victims were said to be "relapsed"; for since the Inquisition was ecclesiastical, it could not shed one drop of blood, and in order to do lip service to the rules, the prisoners were said to have "fallen away" and were handed over to secular justice. Burning them at the stake prevented the profuse bloodletting of other measures. I leave Your Mercies to judge the unholy logic of that process.

These readings, the abjurations *de levi* and *de vehementi*—lighter and stronger recantations—were met with screams of anguish from those sentenced to unendurable punishment, resignation in others, and the public's approval when the maximum penalty was applied. The priest who denied the presence of Christ in the host was condemned to the stake amid roaring applause and nods of satisfaction. After brutally scourging his hands, tongue, and tonsure as a sign that he was stripped of his sacred orders, his tormentors led him to the stake, which had been set up on the esplanade outside the Puerta de Alcalá. The old woman accused of witchcraft—of too easily finding treasures hidden by fleeing Jews and Moors—was sentenced to a hundred lashes, with the additional punishment of life imprisonment—and little that mattered, for such an elderly lady! A bigamist got off with two hundred lashes and exile for ten years, the first six to be spent rowing in the galleys. Two blasphemers received exile and three years in Oran. A cobbler and his wife, reconciled

Jews, were sentenced to life imprisonment and a *de vehe-menti* abjuration. The twelve-year-old girl, a Judaizer, received a sentence of wearing an identifiable brown habit and serving two years of confinement, at the end of which she would be placed in a home with a Christian family to be instructed in the Faith. Her sixteen-year-old sister, a Judaizer, was condemned to life imprisonment without appeal. Their own father, a Portuguese tanner, had denounced them, under torture; he himself was sentenced to a *de vehementi* abjuration before being burned at the stake. He was the man who had been brought in on muleback because he could not walk. The mother, her whereabouts unknown, would be burned in effigy.

Accompanying the priest and the tanner on their way to the stake were a merchant and his wife, also Portuguese Jews, an apprentice silversmith—clearly a grievous sin—and Elvira de la Cruz. Everyone but the priest recanted in due form, and showed repentance. They would be mercifully garroted before being burned. The grotesque effigy of don Vicente de la Cruz, and those of his two sons, the dead one and the one who could not be found, were set atop long poles. His daughter wore the white sanbenito and conical hat, and in that garb was led before the judges to be read her sentence. With bone-chilling indifference, she recanted, as asked, all the crimes she had committed and would ever commit: being a Judaizer, a criminal conspirator, and violating a sacred place, among other charges. She looked totally forsaken up on that platform, head low, her Inquisitorial robes hanging like a sack over her tortured body. After recanting, she heard her sentence confirmed with resigned apathy. I was moved to pity despite the accusations she had made against me, or had allowed to be made. Poor girl, she was the victim and instrument of brutes without scruples or conscience, however much they paraded their God and their holy faith.

After Elvira was taken away, I saw that it was not long before my turn. The plaza began to whirl before me; I was numb with terror and shame. Desperate, I looked for the face of Captain Alatriste or some friend to find comfort, but I found nothing, not one trace of pity or sympathy. Nothing but a wall of hostile faces, jeering, expectant, sinister. The face a mob adopts when treated to free barbaric spectacles.

But Alatriste saw me. He was again beside one of the columns of the arches, and from there could see the bench where I sat with other penitents, each of us flanked by a pair of constables as mute as stones. Preceding me in the fateful ritual was a barber accused of blasphemy and of making a pact with the Devil—a short, wretched-looking man who sobbed with his face in his hands because no one was going to save him from his hundred lashes and years of flogging fish in the galleys of our lord and king.

The captain moved on a little, placing himself where I could see him if I looked in that direction, but I was not capable of seeing anything, sunk as I was in the torment of my own nightmare. Beside Alatriste, a pillicock garbed in his best was ridiculing those of us on the platform, pointing us out, between gibes, to his companions, and at a certain moment he made some jeering comment about me. Up to that point, the captain's habitual restraint had tempered his impotent rage, but now that anger made him turn, without a moment's reflection and, as if accidentally, swing an elbow into the churl's gut. The man whirled about with an angry frown, but his protest died in his throat when he looked into the gray-green eyes of Diego Alatriste, staring at him with such menacing coldness that he closed up like a tulip at eventide.

Again Alatriste moved on, and as he did, he could better see Luis de Alquézar in his loge. The royal secretary stood out from other officials because of the embroidered cross of Calatrava on his chest. He was in black, and his round head with its feathery hair was rigid atop the starched collar: he might have been a figure in a painting. His clever eyes, however, were darting from side to side, taking in every detail of the events. At times that evil gaze focused on the fanatic countenance of Fray Emilio Bocanegra, and in their sinister immobility his eyes seemed to have communicated perfectly. At that moment and in that place they were the embodiment of true power in that court of venal functionaries and fanatic priests. They acted under the diffident regard of the fourth Hapsburg, who was watching his subjects condemned to the stake without lifting an eyebrow, reacting only to turn from time to time to the queen to explain, behind the cover of a glove or a blue-veined hand, some detail of the spectacle. Elegant, chivalrous, affable, and weak, he was the august plaything of his advisors. Hieratical, incapable of seeing earth, he gazed always toward heaven. Unsuited for bearing upon his royal shoulders the grand heritage of his ancestors, he was dragging us along the road to the abyss.

My fate was beyond remedy, and had the plaza not been swarming with catchpoles, constables, *familiares,* and royal guards, perhaps Diego Alatriste would have done something barbarous, desperate, and heroic. At least I like to believe that he would, given the opportunity. But all was futile; time was running against him and against me. Even should don Francisco de Quevedo arrive, once my custodians pulled me to my feet and led me toward the dais where the sentences were being read, neither our lord and king nor the Pope of Rome could alter my fate. And no one knew what he might bring, in any case, that would alter anything, even should he arrive in the dwindling few seconds.

The captain was agonizing over that very knowledge when he became aware that Luis de Alquézar was looking directly at him. Actually it was impossible to know that, for Alatriste was nearly invisible beneath his hat in the midst of that mob of people. Yet he was sure that Alquézar's eyes had been focused on him; then he saw the royal secretary catch Fray Emilio Bocanegra's eye, and he, as if he had just received a message, turned to scour the crowd. Alquézar slowly lifted one hand to his chest, and he seemed to be searching for someone among the throng to Alatriste's left, for his eyes were fixed on a point there. The hand slowly rose and fell, twice, and the secretary again looked toward the captain. Alatriste turned and sighted two or three hats moving toward the place where he was standing beneath the arches.

The captain's instinct took charge before his mind could analyze the situation. Swords were useless in such a tightly packed crowd, so he readied the dagger he wore at his left side, freeing it from the tail of his short cape. Then he faded back among the spectators. Imminent danger had always given him a clear mind and a practical economy of actions and words. He moved along the row of columns, and saw the hats stop, indecisive, at the spot where he had been. He quickly glanced toward Luis de Alquézar's loge, where the secretary was still scrutinizing the throng below; the rigid impassivity demanded by protocol could not hide his irritation.

Alatriste moved on toward the de la Carne arches and the other side of the plaza, and peered up at the platform from that angle. He could not see me, but he did have a good view of Alquézar's profile. He was grateful that he had not brought his pistol—they were forbidden, and among so many people it was dangerous to move about with one on him—for he might not have been able to suppress the impulse to leap onto the platform and roast the secretary's chestnuts with one shot. *But you* will *die,* he swore mentally, eyes drilling into the royal secretary's despicable face. *And until the day you do, you will remember my visit. You will never sleep easily again.*

They had brought the barber accused of blasphemy to the dais, and were beginning the long relation of his crime and sentence. Alatriste thought he remembered that I came after the barber, and he was trying to edge a little closer so he could see me, when he again caught sight of the hats, now dangerously close. These were obviously tenacious men. One had dropped back, as if to search in a different part of the crowd; but two of them—a black felt and another brown with a long plume—were progressing in his direction, breasting their way through the sea of humanity.

There was no choice but to take cover, so the captain had to give up trying to see me and retreat beneath the arches. He would not have the ghost of a chance among that throng; all anyone had to do was call upon the minions of the Holy Office and every man down to the last idler would join in the chase. The opportunity to slip away was only a few steps farther on: a narrow alley with two sharp turns that led to the Plaza de la Provincia. On days like these, people used the alley to relieve themselves, despite the crosses and saints the residents placed at each corner to discourage that practice. The captain walked in that direction, and just before plunging into the narrow passageway, in which no more than one person could move at a time, he glanced over his shoulder and saw two figures emerging from the crowd, right on his heels.

He did not even venture a longer look. He quickly unfastened his short cape, wrapped it around his left arm to serve as a buckler, and with his right hand unsheathed the *vizcaína*—to the shock of a poor man emptying his bladder at the first turn, who when he saw the weapon, made fumble-fingered attempts to fasten his breeches as quickly as possible. Ignoring him, Alatriste set one shoulder against the wall, which, like the ground, stunk of urine and filth. *A fine place to be knifed,* he thought as he took a tighter grip on the *vizcaína.* A fine place, *pardiez,* to go to hell in good company.

. . .

The first of his pursuers turned into the little alley, and, corralled in that very tight space, Alatriste glimpsed eyes terrified by the gleam of his naked dagger. He even made out a large mustache, shaped like a sword guard, and the thick sidewhiskers of a blustering braggart. Quick as lightning, he bent down and slashed the hamstring of the new arrival. Then in the same upward movement, he slashed his throat. The man fell without time to say "Hail Mary, Mother of . . . ," sprawling in the alley with his life gushing in red spurts from his gullet.

The man behind him was Gualterio Malatesta, and it was a pity he had not been the first. Alatriste needed only a glance at his lean black silhouette to know who he was. In the haste of his pursuit, and then the surprise of the unexpected encounter, the Italian had not yet drawn a weapon, so he jumped back as his companion slumped dying before him, and as the captain lashed out with a slaughterer's swing that missed by a thumb's width. The constriction of the alley left no room for swords, so Malatesta took what cover he could behind his moribund companion. He pulled out his *vizcaína,* and, like the captain, protecting himself with a cape around his arm, engaged Alatriste at close range, crowding him and skillfully dodging and returning thrusts. Daggers ripped cloth, rang on stone walls, brutally targeted the enemy, and neither of the two uttered a word, saving their breath for more deadly purposes. There was still surprise in the Italian's eyes—no *ti-ri-tu, ta-ta* from him this time, the bastard—when the captain's dagger sank into the flesh beneath the improvised shield of Malatesta's cape. His companion, an obstacle between them, was with the Devil now, or well on his way.

The Italian reeled from the wound, and as Alatriste leaned toward him over the fallen man, Malatesta's dagger ripped into his doublet, slicing off buttons and ties as he withdrew it. Arms wrapped in cape and capelet parried thrusts. The men's faces were so close that the captain felt his enemy's breath in his eyes before Malatesta spit into them. The captain blinked, blinded, and that allowed his opponent to land a blow with such force that, had the leather of the buffcoat not slowed it, the dagger would have gone in up to the hilt. As it was, the *vizcaína* sliced through clothing and flesh, and Alatriste felt a chill and a sharp pain when the blade touched his hip bone. Fearing he would faint, he struck at his enemy's face with the grip of his dagger, and blood gushed from the Italian's eyebrows, bathing the scars and craters of his skin and trickling from the tips of his thinly trimmed mustache.

Now the gleam of Malatesta's hard, serpent eyes also reflected fear. Alatriste drew back his arm and stabbed again and again, hitting cape, doublet, air, wall, and finally—

twice—human flesh. Malatesta grunted with pain and rage. Blood was streaming into his eyes as he struck out blindly, dangerous for being so unpredictable. Not counting the blow to his forehead, he had at least three wounds.

They fought for an eternity. Both were exhausted, and the wound in the captain's hip gave him pain, but he was in better shape than Malatesta. It was only a question of time, and the Italian, wild with hatred, resolved to take his enemy with him as he died. It never crossed his mind to ask for mercy, and no one was going to offer it. They were two professionals, aware of what they were doing, sparing with insults and useless words, fighting away for the best and worst they could give. Conscientiously.

Then the third man appeared—he too dressed like a swashbuckler, with a beard and baldric and an array of weapons—at the entrance to the alley. His eyes were like platters when he took in the panorama before him: one man stabbed to death, two still going at each other, and the strip of ground in the alley covered with blood tinting the puddles of urine red.

Stupefied for an instant, he muttered, "Blessed Christ and God Almighty," and then reached for his dagger. He could not get past Malatesta, however, who was barely holding himself up with the help of the wall, or pass the obstacle of the other comrade to reach the captain. Alatriste, at the limit of his strength, seized the opportunity to rid himself of his prey, who was still slashing at empty space. His dagger cut across Malatesta's cheek, and finally he had the satisfaction of hearing a curse in Italian. Then the captain threw his short cape over the third man's *vizcaína*, and fled down the alley toward La Provincia plaza, his breath burning in his chest.

He was soon out the other end of the alley, straightening his clothing as he left. He had lost his hat in the struggle, and had another man's blood on his clothing, while his own was dripping down inside his doublet and breeches. Just to be safe, he headed for the church of Santa Cruz, the nearest haven. He stood quietly at the gate, getting his breath back, ready to dash inside the church at the first hint of trouble. His hip was painful. He pulled his handkerchief from his purse and, after feeling for the wound with two fingers and deciding that it was not grave, stuffed the linen into it. But no one came out of the alley, and no one came looking for him. Everyone in Madrid was immersed in the spectacle of the *auto-da-fé*.

It was almost time for me, and for the poor souls behind me. The inquisitors were, at that moment, sentencing the barber accused of blasphemy to a hundred lashes and four years in the galleys. The poor man was wringing his hands, head bowed, weeping, pleading for mercy that no one was going to grant his wife and four children. In any case, he'd gotten better than the penitents wearing cone hats and riding mules who were on their way to the stakes at the Alcalá gate. Before nightfall they would be grilled to a crisp.

I was next, and I was so desperate and so shamed that I was afraid my legs would fail me. The plaza, the balconies filled with people, the tapestries, the constables and Holy Office *familiares* on either side of me made my head spin. I wanted to die there, right there, with no further formalities, and without hope. I knew already that I was not going to die, but that my punishment would be a long prison sentence, and perhaps rowing in the galleys after I had served the required years. All that seemed worse than death, to the degree that I had come to envy the arrogance with which the recalcitrant priest went to the stake without recanting or asking for clemency. At that moment it seemed easier to die than to go on living.

They were finished with the barber, and I saw one of the inquisitors in his starched white gorget consult his papers and then look at me. Signed and sealed. I took one last peek at the loge of honor, where our lord and king was leaning a little to one side to whisper something into the ear of the queen, who seemed to smile. They were undoubtedly talking about the hunt, or exchanging pleasantries, or who knows what the bloody hell they were saying, while down below them priests were heartily dispatching their subjects. Beneath the arches, the public was applauding the barber's sentence and joking about his tears, licking their lips at the prospect of the next offender.

The inquisitor consulted his papers, looked my way once more, and then made a last review. The sun was beating down on the platform like lead, and my shoulders were burning beneath the heavy cloth of the sanbenito. Finally, the inquisitor gathered up his papers and began his slow march toward the lectern, fatuous and self-satisfied, enjoying the suspense he was creating.

I looked at Fray Emilio Bocanegra, motionless on the raised dais, sinister in his black-and-white habit, savoring his victory. I looked at Luis de Alquézar in his loge, cunning, cruel, the cross of Calatrava dishonored by its place on his chest. At least, I told myself—and it was, God knows, my only consolation—Captain Alatriste is not sitting here beside us.

The inquisitor stood before his lectern, slowly, ceremoniously, preparing to read my name. Just then a caballero dressed in black and covered with dust erupted into the loge of the royal secretaries. He was in mud-spattered traveling clothes, high riding boots, and spurs, and he had the appearance of having ridden—whipping his mounts from post house to post house—without rest. He was carrying a leather lettercase, which he took straight to the royal secretary. I saw that they exchanged a few words, and that Alquézar, taking the lettercase with an impatient gesture, opened it, glanced at it, looked in my direction, then at Fray Emilio Bocanegra, and back to me.

The black-clad caballero turned, and at last I recognized him.

It was don Francisco de Quevedo.

X. UNFINISHED BUSINESS

The fires burned all night long. People stayed very late by the Alcalá gate, even after the penitents were nothing more than calcified bones in a pile of embers and ashes. Rising columns of smoke were stained red in the light of the flames. Occasionally a breeze stirred, carrying to the crowd a heavy, acrid odor of wood and burned flesh.

All Madrid spent the night there, from honest married women, somber hidalgos, and highly respectable people, to the lowest of the low. Street urchins dashed around at the edges of the coals, as constables cordoned off the area. There were vendors galore, and beggars, making hay. And to each and every one, the spectacle seemed holy and edifying—or at least that was the view they affected in public. Poor, miserable Spain, always disposed to overlook bad governance, the loss of the fleet of the Indies, or a defeat in Europe, with merriment—a boisterous festival, a Te Deum, or a few good bonfires—was once again being faithful to herself.

"It is repugnant," said don Francisco de Quevedo.

He was a great satirist, as I have already mentioned to Your Mercies, the consummate Catholic in the mode of his century and his nation, but he tempered all that with his deeply ingrained culture and limpid humanism. That night he stood motionless, frowning, watching the fire. The fatigue of his breakneck journey showed on his face and in his voice. Although in the latter, his weariness sounded as old as time.

"Poor Spain," he added in a low voice.

One of the fires collapsed, sputtering, in a cloud of sparks, illuminating the figure of Captain Alatriste by his side. People burst into applause. The reddish glow lighted the walls of the Augustinian monastery in the distance, and the nearby stone pillory at the crossroads of Vicálvaro and Alcalá roads, where the two friends stood a bit back from the crowd. They had been there since the beginning, quietly talking. They stopped only when, after the executioner made three turns of the rope around Elvira de la Cruz's neck, the brush and wood crackled beneath the novitiate's body. Of all the penitents, the only one burned alive was the priest. He had stood firm until the last, refusing to reconcile before the priest attending him, and confronting the first flames with a serene countenance. It was sad that when the flames reached his knees—they burned him slowly, showing great piety, to allow him time to repent—he broke down, ending his torment with atrocious howls. But, with the exception of Saint Lawrence, no one, as far as I know, attains perfection on the grill.

Don Francisco and Captain Alatriste had been talking about me. I was sleeping, exhausted and at last free, in our lodgings on Calle del Arcabuz, under the maternal care of Caridad la Lebrijana. I'd fallen into a deep sleep, as if I needed—which was in fact the case—to reduce my adventures of recent days to the confines of nightmare. And while the fires burned at the site of the stakes, the poet had been telling the captain the particulars of his hurried and dangerous journey to Aragon.

The course suggested by Olivares had mined pure gold. Those four words that don Gaspar de Guzmán had written in the Prado meadows—*Alquézar. Huesca. Green Book*—had been enough to save my life and hobble the royal secretary. Alquézar was not only our enemy's surname, it was also the name of the town in Aragon in which he had been born. And to that town don Francisco de Quevedo had hastened, changing post horses along the *camino real*—one dropped stone-dead in Medinaceli—in his desperate attempt to win the race against time. As for the green book, which was what the birth registry was called, it contained

the catalogues, family genealogies, and listings kept by in-
dividuals or parish priests, and records that served as proof
of ancestry.

As soon as don Francisco arrived there, he used his in-
genuity, his famous name, and the money provided by the
Conde de Guadalmedina to sniff through the local archives.
And there, to his surprise, relief, and joy, he found confir-
mation of what the Conde de Olivares already knew
through his private spies: Luis de Alquézar himself *did not
have pure blood.*

In Alquézar's genealogy—as in that of half of Spain—
there was a Jewish branch, this one documented as having
converted in 1534. Those ancestors of Hebrew origin dis-
qualified the royal secretary's claim of nobility. But in a
time in which even purity of blood was bought at so much
per grandfather, that history had been very conveniently
forgotten when necessary proof and documents were created so that Luis de Alquézar could assume a high post at
court. And as, in addition, he commanded the distinction
of being a caballero of the order of Calatrava, which group
did not admit any man who could not prove he was an old
Christian and whose forebears had not defiled themselves
in the practice of manual labors, the falsified documenta-
tion and the conspiracy to provide them were flagrantly il-
legal. Publication of that information—a simple sonnet by
Quevedo would have sufficed—backed by the green book

the poet had obtained in Alquézar's parish in exchange for a weighty roll of silver *escudos*, would have destroyed the royal secretary's reputation, resulting in the loss of his Calatrava habit, his post at court, and the greater part of his privileges as a caballero and man of substance.

Of course, the Inquisition and Fray Emilio Bocanegra, like Olivares himself, were already aware of all this, but in a venal world built upon hypocrisy and spurious manners, the powerful, the carrion-feeding buzzards, the envious, the cowards, and all swine in general, tended to look out for one another. God our Father created them, and in our unhappy Spain they had clung together forever, with great rewards.

"What a pity that you did not see his face, Captain, when I showed him the green book." The poet's quiet voice shouted his fatigue. He was still wearing the dust-covered clothing and bloodstained spurs of his journey. "Luis de Alquézar turned whiter than the papers I put in his hands, then he turned as red as fire, and I feared he was going to collapse of apoplexy. But I had to get Íñigo out of there, so I pressed even closer and said, 'Señor Secretario, there is no time for discussion. If you do not intervene on the lad's behalf, you are lost.' And he did not even try to argue. That great scoundrel recognized that one day every man among us must settle accounts with the All-Powerful."

It was true. Before the scribe could speak my name, Alquézar shot out of his loge like a musket ball, with a dispatch that said a great deal for his qualifications for the post of royal secretary—and any other matter that concerned him. He stopped before a stupefied Fray Emilio Bocanegra, with whom he exchanged a few words in a very low voice. The Dominican's face had shown, in quick succession, surprise, anger, and dismay. His vengeful eyes would have struck don Francisco de Quevedo dead on the spot, had the poet—exhausted from the journey, on pinpoints because of the danger still threatening me, and determined to carry through to the end even if that meant there on the spot—given a fig for all the murderous looks in the world. Wiping sweat from his brow with his handkerchief, again as pale as if the barber had bled him too liberally, Alquézar slowly returned to the loge where the poet was waiting. And finally, over the royal secretary's shoulder, Quevedo watched as on the dais of the inquisitors, Fray Emilio Bocanegra, shaking with spite and rage, motioned to the scribe. After listening respectfully for a few instants, that same scribe took the sentence he was about to read and set it aside, pigeonholing it forever.

Another pyre collapsed with a great crash, and a rain of sparks flooded the darkness, heightening the radiance that illuminated the two men. Diego Alatriste stood unmoving beside the poet, never taking his eyes from the flames. Beneath the brim of his hat, his strong mustache and aquiline nose seemed to make even leaner a face already emaciated by the fatigue of the day, as well as the new wound to his hip. Though not serious, it was quite painful.

"A pity," murmured don Francisco, "I did not arrive in time to save her as well."

He nodded toward the nearest pyre, and seemed shamed by Elvira de la Cruz's fate. Not in regard to himself, or the captain, but by everything that had led the poor girl to this point, destroying her family along with her. Shamed, perhaps, by the land in which he had been fated to live: vengeful, cruel, dazzling in its sterile grandeur but indolent and vicious in everyday life. Quevedo's honesty and stoic, sincerely Christian, Seneca-inspired resignation were not enough to console him. It seemed that to be lucid and Spanish would forever be coupled with great bitterness and little hope.

"At any rate," Quevedo concluded, "it was the will of God."

Diego Alatriste did not immediately reply. God's will or the Devil's, he remained silent, eyes on the fires and the black outlines of the constables and masses of people silhouetted against the ominous backdrop of the flames. He had not yet come to see me on Calle del Arcabuz, though

Quevedo, and then Martín Saldaña, whom they had scouted out earlier in the day, had told him that there was nothing to fear. Everything seemed to have been resolved with such discretion that not even the death of the swordsman in the alley had come to light, nor did anyone have news of the injured Gualterio Malatesta. So, as soon as his wound had been bandaged in Tuerto Fadrique's apothecary, Alatriste had gone with Quevedo to the burning at the Puerta de Alcalá. And there he stayed, along with the poet, until Elvira was nothing but bone and ash in the coals of her pyre.

For one moment the captain thought he sighted Jerónimo de la Cruz among the throng, or at least the ghostly shade the elder brother seemed to have become, the one survivor of the slaughtered family. But darkness and the milling crowd had closed back over his muffled face—if it had in fact been him at all.

"No," Alatriste said finally.

He had taken so long to speak that don Francisco was not expecting to hear anything, and he looked at him with surprise, trying to think what he was referring to. But the captain, expressionless, continued to observe the fires. Only later, after a second long pause, did he slowly turn toward Quevedo and say, "God had no part in this."

Unlike the poet's eyeglasses, Alatriste's gray-green eyes did not reflect the light of the bonfires; they were more reminiscent of two pools of frozen water. The last of the flames shed dancing shadows and red hues on his knife-sharp profile.

I was feigning sleep. Caridad la Lebrijana was sitting by the head of the bed, where she had tucked me in after supper and a warm bath in a large tub brought from the tavern. She was watching over me while, by candlelight, she mended some of the captain's linen. Eyes closed, I was enjoying the warmth of the bed, in a delicious half-sleep that also allowed me to keep from answering questions or having to say anything about my recent adventure. The mere thought of it—I could not get the infamous san-benito out of my mind—still ate into me like acid. The warmth of the sheets, the kind company of La Lebrijana, the knowledge that I was among friends, and especially the prospect of lying there in the quiet, eyes closed, as the world outside whirled on with no thought of me, had lulled me into a lethargy resembling happiness, compounded by the thought that during my imprisonment no one had torn a word from me that would incriminate Diego Alatriste.

I did not open my eyes when I heard steps on the stairway, or when La Lebrijana, swallowing an exclamation, threw her mending to the floor and herself into the captain's arms. I lay listening to the quiet murmur of conversation, several resounding kisses from the tavern keeper, the new arrival's mutter of protest, and footsteps receding down the stairs. I thought I was alone until after a long silence I again heard the captain's boots, this time approaching the bed, and stopping there.

I nearly opened my eyes, but did not. I knew that he had seen me in the plaza, humiliated among the penitents. And I had not been able to forget that because I had disobeyed his orders, I had let myself be trapped like a linnet the night we attacked the convent of the Adoratrices Benitas. In short, I still did not find myself strong enough to confront his questions or his reproaches. Not even the silence of his gaze. So I lay motionless, breathing evenly to feign sleep.

There was an endless time during which nothing happened. No doubt he was watching me in the light of the candle La Lebrijana had left by the bed. Not a sound, not his breathing, nothing at all. And then, when I was beginning to doubt that he actually was there, I felt the touch of his hand, the rough palm that he laid for a moment on my forehead, with a warmth and unexpected tenderness. He held it there a moment and then brusquely pulled away. I heard the steps again, and the sound of the cupboard being opened, the clink of a glass and a jug of wine, and the scraping of a chair being moved.

Cautiously, I opened my eyes. In the dim light of the room I saw that the captain had unfastened his doublet and unbuckled his sword. Seated by the table, he was drinking in silence. The wine gurgled again and again as it was poured into the glass. He drank slowly, methodically, as if he had nothing else in the world to do. The yellowish candlelight illuminated the light blotch of his shirt, the plane of his face, his short-trimmed hair, the tip of his thick soldier's mustache. He was silent, not moving except to drink. Behind him was the window he had opened, and I could see vague outlines of nearby rooftops and chimneys. Over them shone a single star, still, silent, cold. Alatriste stared fixedly into the void, or at his own ghosts wandering in the darkness. I knew his eyes when the wine clouded them, and I could guess how they looked at that moment: glaucous, absent. At his waist, blood was slowly soaking the bandage on his hip, staining his white shirt with red.

He seemed as resigned and alone as the star winking outside in the night.

Two days later, sun was shining on Calle de Toledo, and again the world was wide and filled with hope, and the vigor of youth was leaping in my veins. Sitting at the door of the Tavern of the Turk, practicing my penmanship

with the writing materials Licenciado Calzas kept bringing me from La Provincia plaza, I was again seeing life
with that optimism and that speedy recovery following
misfortune that only good health and youth can give.
From time to time I looked over toward the women selling
vegetables in the stands across the street, the hens pecking
scraps, and the ragamuffins running around among the
horses and coaches, as I listened to the sound of conversations inside the tavern. I considered myself the most con-
tented boy in the world. Even the verses I was copying
seemed to me the most beautiful ever written.

The shadow that comes to end day's reverie
Will bring the dark, and close my eyelids fast,
Enabling this soul of mine, at last,
To slough off anguish and anxiety.

The words were don Francisco de Quevedo's, and they
had seemed so lovely when I heard him casually reciting
them between sips of San Martín de Valdeiglesias, that I
had asked his permission to write them out in my best
hand. Don Francisco was inside with the captain and the
others—the *licenciado*, Dómine Pérez, Juan Vicuña, and
the Tuerto Fadrique—all of them celebrating with carafes
of the finest, sausages and cured hares, the happy end to a
bad situation, which no one mentioned explicitly but all

had very much in mind. One after another they had ruf-
fled my hair or given me an affectionate pinch on the
cheek as they arrived at the tavern. Don Francisco brought
me a copy of Plutarch so that I could practice my reading.
The *dómine* brought a silver rosary, Juan Vicuña came
with a bronze belt buckle he had worn in Flanders, and
the Tuerto Fadrique—who was the pinchpenny of the
brotherhood and little inclined to part with his money—
brought an ounce of a compound from his pharmacy that
he assured me was perfect for building up the blood and
restoring color to a lad like myself, who had suffered so
many recent travails. I was the most honored, and the hap-
piest, boy in all the Spains, as I dipped one of Licenciado
Calzas's good goose quills into the inkwell, and continued:

That darkness, though, will not leave memory
On that far shore where once it brightly blazed,
Instead, my flame will burn through icy waves
To flout the laws of death's finality.

It was at that verse when, as I looked up again, my
hand stopped in midair and a drop of ink fell onto my page
like a tear. Up Calle de Toledo came a very familiar black
coach, one with no escutcheon on the door and a stern
coachman driving the two mules. Slowly, as if in a dream,
I set aside paper, pen, ink, and drying sand, and stood

rooted as if the carriage were an apparition that any wrong movement on my part might dispel. As the coach pulled up to where I stood, I saw the little window, which was open, with the curtains unfastened. First I saw a perfect white hand, and then the blond curls and the sky-blue eyes that Diego Velázquez later painted: the girl who had led me to within a breath of the gallows. And as the carriage rolled past the Tavern of the Turk, Angélica de Alquézar looked straight at me, in a way—I swear by all that is holy—that sent a chill from the tip of my spine to my bewitched and furiously pounding heart. On an impulse, without considering what I was doing, I placed my hand on my chest, honestly and truly lamenting that I was not wearing the gold chain with the amulet that she had given me to ensure a sentence of death, and which, had the Holy Office not taken it from me, I swear by Christ's blood I would have continued to wear around my neck with besotted pride.

Angélica understood the gesture. Her smile, that diabolic expression I so adored, lighted her lips. And then with a fingertip, she brushed them in something very like a kiss. And Calle de Toledo, and Madrid—the entire sphere— vibrated with a delicious harmony that made me feel jubilantly alive.

I stood watching, still as stone, long after the carriage disappeared up the street. Then, choosing a new quill, I smoothed the point against my doublet and finished putting down don Francisco's sonnet.

Soul, in which a godhead was enclosed,
Veins, through which a humor's fire arose,
Marrow, the seat of earthly passion's reign,

Will fly the body, but quiddity retain;
Though ash, they will have sensibility,
Be dust enamored through eternity.

It was growing dark, but not yet dark enough for a lantern. The Posada Lansquenete was situated on a filthy, stinking street derisively called Calle de la Primavera—though there was no perfume of springtime there! It was near the Lavapiés fountain, the location of the lowest taverns and wine cellars in Madrid, as well as of its most ruinous brothels. Clothes were drying on lines strung from one side of the street to the other, and through open windows came the noise of quarrels and crying babies. Horse droppings were piled at the entrance to the inn, and Diego Alatriste took care not to soil his boots when he went into the corral-like courtyard where a broken-down cart with no wheels, only bare axles, was set up on stones. After a quick glance around, he took the stairs, and after thirty or so steps, and after four or five cats had darted between his legs, he reached the top floor without challenge.

Once there, he studied the doors along the gallery. If Martín Saldaña's information was correct, it was the last door on the right, just at the corner of the corridor. He walked in that direction, trying not to make any noise and at the same time gathering up the cape that concealed his buffcoat and pistol. Doves were cooing in the eaves, the only audible sound in that part of the house. From the floor below rose the aroma of a stew. A serving girl was humming something in the distance. Alatriste stopped, glanced around for a possible escape route, assured himself that his sword and dagger were where they should be, then pulled his pistol from his belt and, after testing the primer, thumbed back the hammer. The moment had come to settle unfinished business. He smoothed his mustache, unfastened his cape, and opened the door.

It was a miserable room that smelled of confinement, of loneliness. Some early-rising cockroaches were scurrying across the table among the remains of a meal, like looters after a battle. There were two empty bottles, a water jug, and chipped glasses. Dirty clothes were slung over a chair, a urinal sat in the middle of the floor, a black doublet, hat, and cape hung on the wall. There was one bed, with a sword at its head. And in the bed was Gualterio Malatesta.

A certainty: If the Italian had made the least move of

surprise, or of menace, Alatriste would have without so much as a "Defend yourself!" fired the pistol he held at point-blank range. Instead, Malatesta lay staring at the door as if he were struggling to recognize who had come in, and his right hand did not make a twitch in the direction of the pistol lying ready on the sheets. He was propped up on a pillow, and a face that could strike terror on its own was made even more frightening by pain, a three days' beard, a badly closed, inflamed wound above his eyebrows, a filthy poultice covering a nasty cut below his left cheekbone, and an ashen pallor. Bandages crusted with dried blood wound around his naked torso, and from the dark stains seeping through them, Alatriste counted a minimum of three wounds. It seemed clear that the assassin had got the worst of the recent skirmish in the alley.

With his pistol still pointed at Malatesta, the captain closed the door behind him and approached the bed. The Italian seemed to have recognized him at last, for the glitter of his eyes, exacerbated by fever, had turned harder, and his hand made a weak attempt to reach for the pistol. He had obviously lost a lot of blood. Alatriste held the barrel of his weapon two inches from the Italian's head, but his enemy was too debilitated to defend himself.

After acknowledging the futility of trying, he simply lifted his head a little off the pillow. Beneath the Italian mustache, now in need of care, appeared the white flash of the dangerous smile the captain, to his misfortune, knew well. Fatigued it is true—and twisted in a grimace of pain—but it was the unmistakable smile with which Gualterio Malatesta seemed always prepared to live or else depart for the lower regions.

"Forsooth!" he murmured. "If it is not Captain Alatriste."

His voice was muffled and weak in tone, though firm in words. The black, febrile eyes were fixed on the visitor, ignoring the barrel of the gun pointed at him.

"It appears," the Italian continued, "that you are performing your charitable works by visiting the ill." He laughed to himself.

For a moment the captain held his glance and then lowered the pistol, though he kept his finger on the trigger. "I am a good Catholic," he replied mockingly.

Malatesta's short dry laugh intensified when he heard that, ending in a fit of coughing. "I have heard that." He nodded, when he had recovered. "Yes, that is what they say. Although in recent days there have been some yeas and nays on the subject."

He still held the captain's eyes, but then, with the hand that had not been capable of picking up the pistol, he motioned toward the jug on the table.

"If it is not too much, would you set that water a little

closer? Then you could boast that you had also given drink to the thirsty."

Alatriste considered for a moment, then picked up the jug and brought it to the bed, never taking his eyes from his enemy. Malatesta drank two avid gulps, observing the captain over the rim of the jug.

"Have you come to kill me straight off," he inquired, "or do you hope that first I will spill out the details of your most recent venture?"

He had set the jar to one side, and weakly swiped his mouth with the back of his hand. His smile was the smile of a cornered snake: dangerous to the last hiss.

"I have no need for you to tell me anything." Alatriste shrugged. "It is all very clear: the trap at the convent, Luis de Alquézar, the Inquisition. Everything."

"The Devil. You have simply come to kill me, then."

"That is so."

Malatesta studied the situation. He did not seem to find it promising.

"And the fact that I have nothing new to tell you," he concluded, "only shortens my life."

"More or less." Now it was the captain who flashed a hard, dangerous smile. "Although I shall do you the honor of assuming that you are not a man to spill your guts," he said, with some irony.

Malatesta sighed, shifting painfully as he felt his bandages.

"Very chivalrous on your part." Resigned, he pointed to the sword at the head of his bed. "A pity that I am not well enough to return your courtesy and save you having to kill me in my bed like a dog. But you trimmed my candle quite thoroughly the other day in that accursed alley."

He moved again, attempting to find a more comfortable position. At that moment he did not seem to hold more rancor than was required by their profession. But his dark, feverish eyes were alert, watching Alatriste.

"You truly did . . . I hear that the boy's skin was saved. Is that true?"

"It is."

The assassin's smile widened.

"That pleases me, by God. He is a brave lad. You should have seen him that night at the convent, trying to hold me at bay with a dagger. Hang me if I enjoyed taking him to Toledo, and less, knowing what awaited him. But you know how it goes. He who pays, commands."

His smile had become mocking. Once or twice he looked out of the corner of his eye at his pistol, lying on the sheets. The captain had no doubt that he would use it if the opportunity arose.

"You," said Alatriste, "are a whoreson and a viper."

Malatesta looked at him with what seemed to be sincere surprise.

"*Pardiez,* Captain Alatriste. Anyone who heard you would take you for a Clarist nun."

Silence. Keeping his finger on the trigger of the pistol, the captain took a long look around. Gualterio Malatesta's lodgings reminded him too much of his own for him to be totally indifferent. And in a certain way, the Italian was right. They were not all that far apart.

"Is it true that you cannot move out of that bed?"

"By my faith, no." Malatesta was now looking at him with renewed attention. "What is it? Are you looking for an excuse?" Again the white, cruel smile grew wider. "If it helps, I can tell you of the men I have dispatched posthaste, without giving them time for a 'God help me.' Awake, asleep, from the front, from the back—and more of the second than the first. So don't come to me now with a crisis of conscience." The smile gave way to a quiet little laugh, discordant, evil. "You and I are professionals."

Alatriste looked at his enemy's sword. The guard had as many nicks and dents as his own. *Everything comes down to how the dice fall,* he told himself.

"I would be grateful," Alatriste suggested, "if you would try to grab the pistol, or that sword."

Malatesta stared at him, hard, before slowly shaking his head no.

"Not a chance. I may lie here filleted, but I am no coward. If you want to kill me, press that trigger and it will be over. With luck, I will reach hell in time for dinner."

"I do not like the role of executioner."

"Then shove it up your ass. I am too weak to argue."

He lay his head back on the pillow and closed his eyes, whistling his *ti-ri-tu, ta-ta,* as if the matter had been settled. Alatriste stood with his pistol in hand, as through the window came the distant tolling of church bells.

Finally, Malatesta stopped whistling. He ran his hand over his swollen eyebrows, then across his pocked and scarred face, and again looked at the captain.

"Well? What have you decided?"

Alatriste did not answer. The situation verged on the grotesque. Not even Lope would have dared put such a scene in a play, for fear that the cobbler Tabarca's *mosqueteros*— those toughest critics—would stomp their feet in disapproval. He walked a little closer to the bed, studying his enemy's wounds. They stank, and looked very bad.

"Oh, but make no mistake," said Malatesta, believing he knew what Alatriste was thinking. "I will come out of this. We men from Palermo are tough. So just get it over with."

Diego Alatriste wanted to dispatch the dangerous swine, who had been such a menace in his life and that of his friends. Leaving him alive was as suicidal as keeping a venomous serpent in the room where he planned to sleep.

He wanted and he needed to kill Gualterio Malatesta. Not this way, however, but with steel in their hands, face to face, hearing the gasping and grunts of the fight, and the death rattle at the end.

Thinking it over, he reflected that there was really no hurry. After all, however much the Italian insisted, the two of them were not the same. Perhaps they were in God's eyes, or the Devil's, or man's, but not deep inside, not in their consciences. They were equals in everything except the way they read the dice on the table. Equals, except that if the roles were reversed, Malatesta would have killed Diego Alatriste long before this, while the captain stood there with his sword sheathed, the finger on the trigger of his pistol indecisive.

The door opened, and a woman appeared on the threshold. She was still young, dressed in a blouse and dirty gray petticoats. She was carrying a basket of clean sheets and a demijohn of wine, and when she saw an intruder there she choked back a scream, sending a frightened look to Malatesta. The demijohn fell to the floor, bursting inside the woven wicker covering. She was too frightened to move or speak, and anguish filled her eyes. With one glance, Diego Alatriste knew that her fear was not for herself but for the fate of the badly wounded man on the bed. *After all*, the captain thought, ridiculing himself as he did, *even serpents seek companionship.*

He looked the woman over, taking his time. She was a spindly thing, common looking. Her youth was wearing thin, and only a certain class of life could have imposed the circles of fatigue beneath her eyes. *Pardiez.* She reminded him a little of Caridad la Lebrijana.

The captain looked at the broken demijohn, at the wine spreading like blood across the floor tiles. Then he bowed his head, carefully released the hammer of the pistol, and placed it in his belt. He did everything very slowly, as if he feared he might forget something, or as if he were thinking of something else. And then, without a word or a backward glance, he moved the woman gently aside and left the room stinking of loneliness and defeat. A room too like his own, like all the places he had known throughout a lifetime.

As soon as he was out on the gallery, he began to laugh, and he kept laughing as he went down the stairs to the street, fastening his cape. He laughed as Malatesta had laughed once near the royal castle, in the rain, when he came to tell me good-bye after the adventure of the two Englishmen.

His laugh, like the Italian's, echoed long after he had gone.

EPILOGUE

It seems that war is flaring up again in Flanders, and that most of the officers and soldiers in Madrid have decided to leave and join their *tercios,* seeing what little action there is here and what opportunity there is there for booty and benefits. It has been four days since the Tercio Viejo de Cartagena left with its drums and banners. It was, as you, my reader, undoubtedly know, reformed after the loss of lives suffered two years ago that terrible day in Fleurus. Nearly the entire company are veteran soldiers, and great news is expected from the rebellious provinces.

On a different subject, yesterday, Monday, the chaplain of Las Adoratrices Benitas, Padre Juan Coroado, was killed in a mysterious manner. This priest came from a well-known Portuguese family. He was young, handsome in his person and eloquent in the pulpit. It seems he was standing at the gate of his parish church when a young masked man approached and without speaking a word ran him through with one thrust. There are whispers of women, or vengeance. The killer has not been found.

—*from José Pellicer's weekly bulletin to friends*

To Captain Alatriste

The bards, throughout the ages, have conveyed
Your story, from Homer on, your praises they declare,
And still today antagonists despair
When they recall the fury of your blade.

Breda, Ostend, Maastricht, Antwerp as well,
Were theaters for your exploits, each heroic deed,
Where, sword flashing, you were always in the lead
To serve the King, and his enemy repel.

Lutherans, contentious French, insurgent Flemish,
Dread Turks, Dutchmen, the ever-present English,
All served to help you win your well-earned fame,
Then let the heavens and the earth proclaim
The much-sung feats of a true warrior:
Alatriste! The thunderbolt of war!

To a Certain Priest Petitioner
Much Admired at Court

Lascivious Padre, salacious, and promiscuous,
Would it not serve you better to be religious?
Should there not be one honest woman
To whom you have not promised heaven
Through the attention of your pillicock?
Must you skewer every ewe among your flock?
That sacred staff of yours, your treasure,
You must find raw, abraded beyond measure
From its constant state of excitation
And unrelenting quest of penetration.
Yea, for every virgin you confess
There is another cunny to be blessed.

FROM THE BENEFICIADO VILLASECA

In Faint Praise of the Head Constable, Martín Saldaña

Señor Saldaña, by my faith,
You amble at an ox's pace
When you are summoned to untangle
Some imminently mortal wrangle.
Why then should I be amazed
—Given you're forever dazed—
That meeting with your deputies
May take a few eternities?
Poor ox, his wife doth dally 'round
And Saldaña's head with antlers crown.
But in the end, if I'm not daft,
And precedent reliable,
An ox become a constable
Will wear the horns and get the shaft.

He Ponders That in Youth's Exuberance There Is Need for Providence

Happy, he scales the towering obelisk,
This lad who puts his trust in youthful fire,
Weighing challenge against his heart's desire,
And pitting courage against the gravest risk.

All too rashly, he lifts his wings in flight.
And, a new Icarus, soars near
But does not reach the blazing sphere
That radiates life's daring from the height.

Patrician brio cannot be denied.
Spurred by the ardent blood of youth
The noble spirit ever seeks the prize.

But in this fall to earth may lie a truth.
The prudent voice will serve as surest guide:
The hero is not the valiant, but the wise.

BY DON FRANCISCO DE QUEVEDO

Abiding Love, Beyond Death

The shadow that comes to end day's reverie
Will bring the dark, and close my eyelids fast,
Enabling this soul of mine, at last,
To slough off anguish and anxiety.

That darkness, though, will not leave memory
On that far shore where once it brightly blazed,
Instead, my flame will burn through icy waves
To flout the laws of death's finality.

Soul, in which a godhead was enclosed,
Veins, through which a humor's fire arose,
Marrow, the seat of earthly passion's reign,

Will fly the body, but quiddity retain;
Though ash, they will have sensibility,
Be dust enamored through eternity.

Arturo Pérez-Reverte

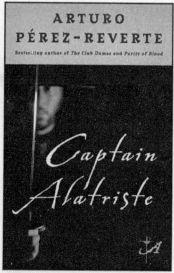

978-0-452-28711-2 / 0-452-28711-1
$14.00 / $20.00 CAN.

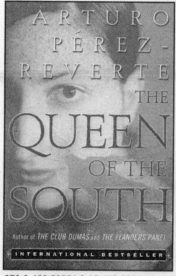

978-0-452-28654-2 / 0-452-28654-9
$14.00 / $20.00 CAN.

Captain Alatriste is the first in a magnificent series of historical novels featuring the adventures of a seventeenth-century Spanish soldier who lives as a swordsman-for-hire.

A perfect blend of suspense and literary ambition, *The Queen of the South* is an explosive story that encompasses sensuality, cruelty, love, and betrayal as its heroine's story unfolds.

Available wherever books are sold.

Plume
A member of Penguin Group (USA) Inc.
www.penguin.com

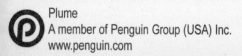